"A novel full of art and magic; sex, murder and love, The Day and Night Books of Mardou Fox casts a spell on the reader. Nisi Shawl tells the moving tale of a writer's life, rich with insight and meaning, pain and pleasure. A short book, but not a small book."

—Victor LaValle, author of **Lone Women**

"Step back, Kerouac! I loved this fabulist reckoning with the legacy of the Beats from the perspective of an overlooked member of their circle: a singular black writer who is no one's muse. Shawl's generous gifts bring 'Marlene Todd,' a.k.a. 'Mardou Fox,' to complex vibrancy in a brilliant act of literary comeuppance."

—Alaya Dawn Johnson, World Fantasy Award-winning author of **Trouble the Saints**

Cover art and design by Bizhan Khodabandeh

Rosarium Publishing
P.O. Box 544
Greenbelt, MD 20768-0544

www.rosariumpublishing.com

THE DAY & NIGHT BOOKS OF MARDOU FOX

Nisi Shawl

To Aunt Cookie,
a sharp Black Beat

Glimmer

August 25 1941   Mama gave me this book for school, but I am using it for my own secrets, and let her and my teacher think I lost it when it is time for me to do my class homework, so that I will have to use just scraps and drawer liner. Those are fine for that. Because I am nearly 10 years old, and mature for my age. Mature enough to have secrets, and a secret diary. I know the perfect place where to hide this. I will get it out and write in it every day I can. Esther and Clarice won't ever figure it out. No, not ever!

August 26 1941   So far, so good. I decided to wrap this little book up in that stupid raggedy shower cap Miss Purdie has been keeping in her bathroom and hasn't ever used and wasn't going to, because if she wants to get clean she just washes up in the sink or maybe in the summer takes a bath. But not a shower. I don't ever hear that running.

But why am I wasting my time on her? Here's what's important: My name is Marlene Bianca Todd. I am nine-and-three-quarters years old, and although I'm not as fairskinned as Clarice, I have good hair from our Daddy who is an Indian. And I am skinny but I can fight, though I am no longer the best fighter in my grade since Theresa Olden pinned me to the retaining wall by the football field. But I am going to be the best at something. I swear it.

I have four sisters, but only Esther and Clarice live here—the address is 1624 Ridge Avenue Number 5. Wanda is staying with Gramma Jerry in California. She's too little to send us letters, so we get crayon pictures with notes from Gramma on the back. I have to say she is a very neat colorer. Marian is old enough for her own apartment. She works as a secretary in New York. She will get me a job when I graduate if I want she says, but I don't see her a lot. Mom is mad at her for something about bulls. Which I'm guessing has to do with sex, because otherwise why not explain it when I ask?

That is my family. Daddy is in a rest home because his mind is messed up. Maybe Clarice's has the same issue. But not me.

Number 5 is one half of the top floor of a kind of falling-down apartment house. The most artistic thing about this place is the view.

Now I better go pick some string beans.

August 27 1941   That was close! Esther came around the house corner while I was shoving back the brick to cover up my hiding place. I had to pretend I was taking measurements for a project for school, even though classes won't even start for another week. Esther believed me, though, since she knows I care about getting all *A*s. So then I had to make up what the project was. For science, I said—because she hates science—I was trying to determine building materials expansion rates and contractions for day and night times. And that made her get bored and leave me alone.

I thought she had forgotten the whole thing. But this morning over grits she was showing off for Mama— Heaven only knows why she expected Mama to pay any attention while she was getting ready for work—and

11

started in asking me what I found out. I explained as smartmouth as I could that I only set up my experiment yesterday and would collect my results over the next twenty-four hours. Then I began to lay out a graph on the inside of a flour bag from the trash, but now Mom WAS paying attention and wanted to know where my notebook (this one) had gone so I had to tell that story, too.

Lying is more work than it is worth. It makes me so tired.

Nevertheless I will have to keep getting up all night to check on my experiment that doesn't even exist, or Esther will realize I am still next to her in bed, and even though it's still summer, when the sun goes down it gets COLD on the porch we sleep on. I am not looking forward to this in the least.

August 28 1941   What happened

September 2 1941   First day of school. I can start all over ~~and ignore~~ in a way, because even though I know most of these kids from fifth and some of them played with us during the summer this is fall and sixth grade now, in an entirely new building. We're middle school kids, me and Clarice. ~~And I found out~~ And Marian sent me a blouse and skirt she can't wear anymore, and money to buy a purse, though I had to use that for bigger shoes instead. Mama blames how much they grew on me going barefoot. We had a good time anyway shopping Saturday. I thought she would let me have the patent leather even at one point.

And it's no use. I can't keep secrets from myself. I have to write about it. Somehow.

I am not really a good scientist. You need a theory and I don't have one. I'm more like a magazine reporter. I'll tell this like a story for *Ebony* and figure it out afterwards. I'll use drawings to illustrate it because we haven't got any camera.

It was the night of August 27, 1941. The sky had barely gotten dark by our bedtime. Luckily this was my turn to sleep on the outside of the bed. Usually that's the worst—you get pushed out and the blankets don't stretch far enough. But being on the outside I could put

Daddy's watch on the floor, easy to reach, and it had a radium dial, so not having electricity on the porch didn't matter for my experiment. I put the flashlight by the watch, only to save batteries I wasn't going to switch it on in the apartment.

Esther expected me to check my wall measurements every hour. I said no, I only had to do it five more times: midnight and four a.m. and eight a.m. and noon and four p.m. I had already checked at eight p.m. right before we got in our pjs and put down the dimensions on my graph. I made sure she saw that and how I copied my ruler's marks, too.

If this was a scary book it would have happened at midnight. But nothing was weird then. I went into the living room and Mama was breathing steady, and her alarm clock dial glowed with enough light to see the door out by. Then out to the hallway and the flashlight worked fine, and I took the stairs past number 3 quietly as I could so Miss Purdie wouldn't complain to Mama about me waking her up. But I heard her talking loud to one of her friends and laughing, so then I just walked normally. And everything was normal, and I made my fake measurements and came back up.

Seemed like I was hardly warm again under the covers when I woke up knowing it was 4. I have a good sense of time. Now Mama was snoring. No sounds were coming out of Miss Purdie's place this time. I did what I said I would and then

And then I noticed. Noticed what? A lot of things all at once. That the crickets had stopped. And the wind wasn't blowing any longer. And that my feet were floating and I was not actually touching the ground. I was close but not quite ON it.

I felt so frightened. My stomach and everything felt empty and awful. I reached out with one hand to catch hold of the side of the apartment house and it was a big relief when I could touch it! I started pulling myself around to the front door. I don't know what was I thinking. That I would bob up to our floor like a birthday balloon and climb in bed and gradually sink down onto the mattress like when the helium leaks out?

Next I heard the music. No, that's not the right word. Not exactly heard it. The best way to say this is to say that I heard where the music would fit if it was solidly, truly real. Like that box Gramma Jerry has for silverware with velvet holes for forks and spoons. I heard those holes. They were for trumpets and drums and guitars and pianos. It was sad and grand. Majestic is how it seemed to me.

Over the top of the roof rose the face of a lady shining like a golden moon. I was done being afraid—at least for the moment. The lady's face was kind and beautiful.

That's what the lady looked like. She saw me and smiled. She opened her big lovely mouth. She called me by my name.

"Marlene. Sweet Marlene—I remember!" Sort of as if she was bending over she came nearer. "You will! You're going to—" She quit talking and turned like she was looking behind her and pulled back. Far enough I could see the top part of her clothes: a white shirt with the kind of collar men wear. And she had a thing like a cross on a ribbon or something around her neck. But not a cross like Miss Purdie's.

That's it in detail. As best as I can remember it.

"Okay," said the lady, not looking at me. She went away, and suddenly I was terrified! All alone in the dark and I had dropped the flashlight! I grabbed out and found the door handle and opened the door and heard it hit something that rolled away. Which of course was the flashlight, and now that had stopped working and I couldn't find it right away, so I gave up. Halfway up the steps I realized my feet were resting on them like usual. One creaked real loudly under my weight. In the living room Mama stopped snoring. But I could see by the clock she was on her side with her face toward the couch cushions. I snuck past the same as I did at midnight.

I got back in by nudging Esther out of my space and toward the middle. She woke up a little. Enough to say something with her mouth most of the way shut so I couldn't quite hear it, and to put one arm over my shoulder and the other up to touch her hand to my hair.

Right before I fell asleep I realized the impressions of the music notes were getting softer? thinner? Not so deep. Yeah. They were filling up like wet sand smooths out on the beach after you walk on it. The quiet became more and more ordinary.

I only slept a couple of hours. Like I had planned, I got up in plenty of time for my eight o'clock measurements. But my graph and pencils weren't under the bed, because I had forgotten them downstairs. And that made me frightened again, because when I woke up I had been thinking the weird not-music and lady-face and floating were a dream. Not unless I was moving stuff around with my mind.

In the living room Mama was up of course, and her blankets folded and stacked on the couch. She stopped sleeping in the bedroom last year when Daddy went to the home again and she started her sewing business in there. I heard her back in the kitchen measuring coffee into the percolator. She set it on the stove and smiled at me as I walked past to use the bathroom. "You're gonna have to start getting up earlier next week." The words sound like scolding when I write them down. She wasn't mad, though. "Wake the other girls and come eat," she told me.

I wanted to say I had to collect my data first but I knew better. I needed to put on clothes to go outside anyway. I ran to the porch and pulled off the covers from Esther and Clarice. Their eyes were open but they were too lazy to get up on their own.

And now I have to put this away till after school tomorrow.

September 3 1941   That was long. I read it over again before I started to write this next part, all ten pages. I could change it and make it better. If it was a real article in a magazine, I know it would have lots of differences. It's just practice, so I'll keep on the only way I know how for now, since I'm not even done.

The main part is written. Here's the wrap-up: When I did my next measurements that morning it was 8:08 on Daddy's watch. So I was a few minutes late, but the experiment was fake and that didn't really matter. My ruler was in the grass on our side of the house, the side I had gone around on. I found the graph in the weeds against the bottom of the bushes marking off the yard from the garden. The wind must have blown it there. It was a little wet—just from dew. I patted it dry on my dungarees and recorded my data. Esther came down and watched.

Clarice stuck her head out the kitchen window and called us to breakfast. On the way in I bent over and tried to hide the cracked glass on the front of the flashlight as I picked it up. But Esther saw it anyway. "Oooo! I'ma tell!"

"Tell what?" I acted like everything was fine.

"Tell you broke it!"

I said shut up and reminded her she cut pictures out of that magazine Mama was saving where they talked about Daddy's friends he fought in the war with. Worse than mad, that had made her sad. "Holes," she had kept saying.

Mama left for Mrs. Gilmore's. After we ate I shut myself in what used to be her bedroom. Behind the cracked glass the flashlight's bulb still wouldn't come on. I decided I could save up milk money to buy us a new one if it was dead for good. Probably it will take till Thanksgiving, but I don't like milk anyway. What I tried not to let bother me was that between that and the graph and ruler it looked like something actually happened.

And that is the problem. I wanted to ignore it. Now I changed my mind. I will figure it out. I have written what happened. The truth. I will read it back again and think things over instead of pretending it's all normal and fine.

All by myself.

September 4 1941   The guidance counselor was not supposed to talk. Here's her job: to listen to us kids, even the Negroes, and help us, and not reveal our secrets. I don't have any proof she said something to my teacher and Mama. I'm just sure she did.

Maybe I was stupid to think she'd keep quiet? Who else was I going to ask, though? I had no idea what the floating and the ladymoon meant. I still don't. I mean not the slightest clue. And guidance counselor appointments were already scheduled for everybody as part of beginning sixth grade.

We started off discussing the fact of Clarice being in my same class even though she's a year older and how that was a challenge for me. Miss Johnson asked a lot of questions, mostly about Clarice's "mental state," and her "grasp of reality." And I explained how my sister got behind when she missed some attendance traveling with Daddy and his other wife, and then the school she went to when they settled down in New Mexico a while wasn't very good. Not according to the tests she took when she came to live with us at Christmas break.

So that didn't take long. And then since I had been feeling confused over the other stuff I brought it up. Big mistake.

She thought I was crazy. Like Daddy. Maybe like Clarice, too?

Miss Johnson had me say everything twice. She stopped looking at me and began writing notes. She would smile and put her face in my direction whenever I stopped talking, but looking over my shoulder at the wall. Not directly in my eyes. With white people that means they're lying.

Miss Johnson sent a note for Mama in a sealed envelope so I couldn't read it before Mama did. As I walked down the steps to the door out I saw her go in the teacher lounge.

Mama came home from Mrs. Gilmore's early today so she could make pillows. Now she has to take off tomorrow night too for a meeting with Miss Johnson.

I'm not crazy. Am I?

Clarice isn't either.

September 6 1941   I don't believe I'll have any more chances to write in this book ever again.

Last night Mama took me to the school with her. For the beginning of the meeting I had to wait in a chair in the hall outside Miss Johnson's office. Then Miss Johnson called me in. I sat on the davenport next to Mama and she asked me to explain myself. But I had already made up my mind I wasn't going to say anymore about what happened and in fact would not even admit things I already said. Let Miss Johnson sound nuts. So my mouth stayed shut like I wish hers had. Shut like mine should have during our appointment.

Eventually they gave up trying to get me to talk and sent me back out of the room. Mama came out too only a little later and we walked home. The sky was still light but the sun was gone. I thought about how my favorite time of day is night. Mama reached out and took my hand as we went off the sidewalk to cross Jefferson. We hung on to each other after we reached the other side.

I wasn't rude and staring, but I was able to see Mama's face easy, how her eyelids drooped down almost closed. Sometimes when she's tired they do that, or she's thinking I guess. Sitting at the kitchen table or in front of the sewing machine. But we were moving. We were walking fast to get me home before bedtime. And then she shook her head and made a little muttering sound.

Words I couldn't hear. Then words I could: "I was saving extra for your birthday."

I will be ten the end of November, as I explained earlier. "To get me what?"

I would call the smile she gave me disgusted. "Little Tramp!" She snorted a short snort. She laughed. "Tell you? You'd like that!" she said. It made me feel better to think she might still buy me a present—which was the only reason she would have had not to say what it was. And "Little Tramp" was not an I'm-angry sort of name for any of us girls.

Pretty soon we came to the path to cut through the park past the pond. She sat me down on a log by the water where it wasn't dark. She said we didn't have much time but she needed to tell me things Esther was too young to hear. I wondered about Clarice, who is actually older than me. But only Marian is more mature. And Mama is not Clarice's real mother. That's Daddy's other wife.

After what Mama said about what Miss Johnson said, and that I would have weekly appointments with her and be under her observation until summer vacation, she made me promise that I hadn't been in and wouldn't be in any kind of trouble.

Not on one of these nights since the first time it happened have I seen the ladyface or floated or heard that not real music. Maybe I never will again.

Whether I do or don't, I can't ever get caught writing about it anymore or even thinking about it. I'm not the only one who'll pay. Our whole family would suffer.

So good-bye, book.

Glare

September 7 1953   Man, I wish junk did not make me so sick. Wish I could revel in it like my friends expect of a colored gal. These new ones are inclined to act suspicious till I twist up some tea to smoke. And even then they aren't so sure. ... Because I dress nice outta Marian's closet they think I got more money than I should be makin at my two-bit job.

Which, thanks to Daddy's pension, I do. But I prefer not to talk about that.

This is my second diary I started for this fall. The first disappeared on a night we were hoppin around between clubs and bars and living rooms and basements. I think probably Terry has it, because I remember him asking "Whatchou writin in there, Marlene?" Like colored folk don't know how to use a pen. But I shouldn't say that. He didn't mean nothin bad by it. He knows I'm a true-born intellectual, the equivalent of Monk or Adderley any day.

Proof: he has been tryna fix me up with this buddy of his, the famous Leo Percepied. The bestseller. And yeah, the man is sorta kinda handsome—in a brooding, lost, and sorrow-loaded way. Makin jokes how much older he is than mosta the rest of us like he really thinks that's funny steada sad. Because I believe in goin my own way I do my best to look past him when he shows up and I'm talkin to someone else, but it's obvious I am a mountain he believes he somehow has to climb. Man, them eyes! Bright on top on the surface, but deep deep black beyond. ... I better not fall in.

September 8 1953   See, I <u>knew</u> it. Quotin to me my own goddam poem. Dark sparkle eyes I had to meet, cause he was speakin to <u>me</u>, sayin my lines: "Breathin up a light beam/Dippin down a breeze/All the air is fine and rare and sippin gold is how we spend it/Sunny after/noons." I broke it off first. Had to. He wasn't gonna. I switched my long hard stare over to Terry, who looked guilty as all get out.

I mashed my lips together tight. Then I said, low, "I want it back."

"What?" Actin like he had no idea what I meant.

"My diary. Where I wrote that poem your friend was just recitin."

Yeah, Terry took it. But he claimed he didn't have it no more. He had handed it over to his pal. Percepied. Who sat there lotus-legged on Adam Moorad's living room floor and grinned at me and drank wine like he was celebratin victory, like he won a bet.

Maybe he did. I was talkin right to him now. "When are you gonna give it back?" I asked him.

He kept a hold on me with his eyes. "When you take it." Issuin a dare. And then scowlin and lookin away and swiggin down half a bottle of red. And then offering the bottle to me without wiping off the mouth. I sipped at it to show I wasn't scared of his germs. I was plannin to share it with the rest of the crowd, but he put one big hairy hand over mine and pulled it back and finished it.

What I loved was that he didn't even pretend to dry my spit off the greeny glass—in fact he licked it. Winked at me while he did. Wiggled his tongue and eyebrows.

So yeah. I took him home. My place, not his, since he still—get this—he still lives with his mother!

But in the cab here to Paradise Alley he practically fell asleep. Up three flights and then dead to the world. To me. As I write this I can look over at him draped hangin off the sofa, too big to fit. Hawai'ian shirt throat open, head and arms thrown back over the end, rumbly voiced snores and sighs robbing my bachelorette pad of peace.

If there was room I'd join him. No. My wide and lonely bed awaits, white and blue, tucked safe against the studio's further wall.

September 9 1953   Well, he won his trophy. Made a black chick.

To be clear, I liked it fine. He woke up after a couple hours and kept his promise, did what he mimed doin with the wine bottle. And his prick was proportionate, firm, warm, its skin like thick velvet.

But then later this mornin, when we woke together, he had to talk and spoil everything.

It started innocent enough. He wondered what I had for breakfast. Coffee, juice, bread. I got out of bed to fill the percolator, and he followed me to the kitchen in bluejeans and undershirt. Intimated he was surprised. Why?

"I had you figured as a grits-and-chitlins girl."

Hunh. I picked up the knife but really did not know what to say. I mean should I begin with how I am not a "girl" and haven't been since graduating high school five years ago? Or gently inform him how nobody, not even the most dedicated of chitlin-lovers, eats them before lunch? Or discourse at academic length on how not every Negro enjoys rinsing the shit, the literal shit, out of pig intestines and then shoving them boiled down their gullets? To cover my confusion I dug out the loaf and commenced to slicin. By the time I snapped out of it I had done the entire thing.

Naturally, he had been talking the whole while. I had occasionally nodded or shook my head. The coffee was burning. I poured it into cups and apologized for not havin any cream.

Leo assured me he liked it black. Again with the eyebrows.

That was enough. "Listen," I said, "I'd love to, you know, spend the day with you." (It was already after eleven o'clock.) "But my job—This is Wednesday—"

He apologized and gulped down his mug and quickly cleared out. Maybe I embarrassed him.

Good.

September 10 1953   Marian doesn't dig what I see in white people. "Your middle name means white," she teases me sometimes. "'Bianca'—but you ain't white, and you never gonna be white, and why you want to, anyways?" After yesterday I am more drawn to her way of thinking.

She took me out for dinner tonight. Not everywhere serves Negroes, even in New York, but she had Green-

Booked this Chinese restaurant in Brooklyn, the Fulton Palace. Twenty minutes from her office in the Pulitzer Building by subway.

We had the Lo Mein. Beef for me, chicken for her because she was watching her weight. They brought us a plate of those crispy fried rolls for appetizers.

I had found out when I moved in with her from high school how Marian went with women. Didn't bother me; whites for my tastes, women for hers. I rented an apartment of my own soon as I could and we were outta each other's way. She still dressed pretty and had manners to match. Always calm and ladylike.

She tapped the ash off her Winston and listened quietly to my complaints. Said nothin she coulda said about stickin with your own kind. Only asked what I was gonna do next time I run into him.

I shrugged my shoulders. I haven't come up with any good ideas yet. And tomorrow's Friday, when it's likely we'll cross paths.

Maybe he'll be too embarrassed still to show his face.

I changed the subject. "Terry and Adam are talkin about startin a magazine."

My sister smiled and stubbed out her cig. "They publishin your poetry?"

"Of course. And I'm helping them out with the graphics stuff you taught me." I know I sounded defensive. Marian's smiles don't fool me. She's older and seen a few things, she always says, and she knows better who to trust. Certainly not those of the Caucasian persuasion. According to her.

The food came and we ate and talked about where the ad agency's offices were going to relocate now the Pulitzer was actually finally being demolished. I noticed Marian had stopped taking her little pills and instead stirred some drops from a brown bottle into her tea. "Let me see that," I asked her, and she handed over this small vial with a white paper label. Spidery letters spelled out measurements and something in Latin. The first word was *Quercus*, I decided, though the "q" was funny and old-fashioned. Oak. *Quercus glandium spiritus*. Oak gland spirits? Below, in regular printing in a different colored ink, a name and address appeared:

Dr. Dee

230 Summer Place

Brooklyn, New York

GIDneys-1616

"Seein somebody new?"

She nodded. "He ain't tryna 'fix' me to like men. Just keep me off the sauce, help me lose a couple pounds." She took the bottle back and tucked it in her bag. "Been with him two weeks and so far I'm down to 238 from 242." Which didn't sound like much, but I did my best to look impressed. "Maybe you wanna see can he help you? He's cool—long as you ignore how he thinks he can do magic spells and things."

The tray with our checks and fortune cookies came, and they started clearing our plates. Help me with what, I wondered. I don't drink, which is Marian's real problem, and I can take the tea or leave it. It's all for show. When I'm on my own I leave that shit alone. Junk even more so. I hate throwin up.

I didn't say a word. Marian clacked shut the clasp on her purse. "You rather nobody outside the family knows about them dreams?" she asked me. She had seen what I wrote after I graduated from Miss Johnson and come live with her.

"I rather nobody thinks I'm crazy." I picked up the bill, and she snatched it from my hand. I had to make at least a play to pay, but her job's much better than mine and we split the pension with the other three sisters, so we both knew who'd win that contest.

All during the train ride back to Penn and from there across the East River again to the Village, I was what Mama woulda named worry-minded. All mixed up over Leo and the stupid things he had said and how he would act toward me in front of the crowd now we had made it. Plus, I truly prefer not to call those dreams to mind.

September 11 1953   I have decided if I see him tonight to pretend nothing happened.

September 12 1953   Yeah, pretendin didn't last.

First, I thought I would get through the evening without seeing him. Beginning at the Cedar, it was mostly wimmins: Camille and Frankie and Annie and me, joined after we ordered a bowl of chowder and a basket of breadsticks by Terry. No Adam, Leo, or any of that ilk. Then came Roy to lord it over his Annie, and then this painter whose name I don't even know for sure—Julian?—came and sat with us, so three men and four women. And while technically we had the majority, that is just not how this sorta thing works. Roy wanted to cab over to Adam's so he could connect with Carmody, and he insisted we come with him, so we left the bar, but of course, who had any money for cabfare? Nobody, that's who. Roy then broke into a car parked on University, and I do believe he was really gonna steal it. But the owner came, and oh, it's too foolish to describe. But we wound up running—at least

41

it was in the right direction, because by the time we stopped we were almost there.

As we tromped in, Carmody glared like this was his apartment. I got the distinct feeling he and Adam were engaged in some arcane fruity conversation into which the interjections of us four women were not wanted! Camille and Frankie must have felt the same because they soon faded off. But Annie stayed—Roy's arm draped over her in suchaway she had to—and I did, too. Slubborn, as Clarice would say. You need me somewheres, tell me I ain't welcome there.

Leo arrived wearing a ridiculous hat. Well, it would not have looked ridiculous on, say, Lester Young or some other Negro of renown. Black brim and tan crown with a shiny ribbon round it green and yellow like a snakeskin. Flushed red boozeface beneath. How did he manage to look so wrong and yet at the same time so exactly right?

Carmody grinned up at Leo from his chair, his forbidding façade shattering like hard-frozen butter. Annie and the other menfolks wound up in a circle on the floor around my feet.

He said a simple hello. Did not attempt to touch me. All was well. Though I had the feeling he was waiting ... and in a while my feelings were vindicated, for he wandered off from our group to the kitchen in a conversational lull, then called for me: "Marlene! Can you—" He interrupted himself with incoherent cuss words. "Can you help me out here?"

I sat where I was sittin. I mean it was Adam's apartment.

But in a voice like a wounded bull he called me again. And again, and so I went to him. Three times.

In the gleaming kitchen he stood in the farthest corner, hands flat on the maroon countertop, head turned my way. "Hey." I said hey back. At a glance I didn't see anything he oughta need help with.

"Listen," he said. But then he stopped. Itched his nose with one shoulder and kept his hands where they were. "Listen," beginning over, "some stuff you should know about me if we're involved."

"Are we?" I leaned on the doorframe like what we were talking about meant nothin.

He frowned, but not angry. Sad and surprised. "Well, sure. I guess." Eyes puzzling out his hurt.

I took mercy. "All right. We are. So what's this about? You a queen? Or—" remembering Tuesday night— Wednesday morning really "—a switch hitter?"

"What!? NO!!" He glared at his hands and pressed them down hard on the Formica. Now he was angry. "No. But I'm not—look, you gotta let me be me. I'm not the marryin type."

My turn to be surprised. "Marryin? Who said anything about marryin?"

"It's legal here."

"You checked?" Suddenly, I thought about him going to the library, city hall, all that trouble to find out if we could get hitched. That moved me funny. I slouched on into the room, hands in my back pockets and elbows out, a pose I had practiced to look hip. "That's all right, baby. I ain't much on marryin myself," I said. Later for that. First, I need to establish my career.

Meanwhile, I got a diaphragm. I put my arms along Leo's arms and hugged him from behind. He laughed his sweet laugh and turned around and kissed me. Taste of whisky on my tongue. He lifted me up, held me to his chest like a football, mumbled my name, brushed my hairline with his soft lips, ran his nose down my part sniffing me in, and I like to fallen in love. A white man worshippin my hair.

He lowered me to my feet again. I staggered from dizzydom. Then I regained balance and stood tippytoe to plant a smooch on that so-serious chin and waltzed off quick when he grabbed for me. Bumped smack into Roy coming in the doorway, Annie trailing behind him.

I didn't like how Roy looked at me. Like he was ashamed to be caught doin it.

"Terry went to find us a cab," he explained to Leo. Still looking my way. "The bottle Carmody brought's empty, and I'm outta smokes."

We rode home crammed in with him and Annie, and Terry on the floor, and Adam and Carmody, who wanted us to stay with them and hit the tavern. But Leo was on the seat next to me but with his head on my lap, humming loud and buzzing like a big bumblebee against my groin—"Hmmmhmmhmmhmm Hmm Hmm"— to the tune of "Happy Birthday"—nuts as anything, and about to drive me outta my tree! So I insisted and we spent the rest of Friday in bed and a good part of Saturday, too, till Leo said he needed to leave and "get to work." With which sentiment, as you can see, I wholly sympathized.

He'll be back. Bringing what I asked for.

September 13 1953   We had a fight. Or anyhow, an argument.

The plan was to meet at the Cedar around 8:30 or so, eat a whole meal from the menu—Leo said a magazine had paid him, his treat—imbibe and converse till ten and then cut out for my place.

10 p.m. and no sign of him.

11 p.m.

Midnight.

I didn't even have cab fare home. I was hungry—I ate all Frankie's peanuts while she was watchin Adam read his new poem. Leo finally showed up then, the last stanza.

Hours late. And empty-handed.

Terry pulled over a chair from the next table for him, and he crashed down into it. Rocking and laughing, back and forth, side to side. Stoned again.

I thought maybe he had brought my journal in his jacket. I asked. He seemed confused. I tried to make it a joke and stuck my hand inside the nearest pocket I could reach. Something. I pulled it out. A torn-out page with my writing. I choked back a scream. My mauled baby, raggedy edge and crumple up corners and a dirty crease running through its heart, my heart—

I felt his big fingers on the back of my hand, stroking my skin to soothe me, saying shh, shhh, shh, and I realized I wasn't crying, wasn't making any noise at all, so why should he shush me? I stood up. Before I knew where I was headed I stepped onto the stage. Adam had gone. They had turned off the mic and spotlight, but I went on anyway. Read what had been ripped out of my book. I'm copying it:

Softer than summer is the dying:

Decay that's rich with layers of rot,

Mulching awareness of mushrooms sharing

Mycelia yourcelia ourcelia allcelia

The flesh of longing rests

In teeming solitude.

Mists. Mellowness. Ripeness. Reaping.

Where do we find paths for our feet,

These blind clouds bleat?

We fall to rise and roam the skies

Till on a distant shore we beat

Recede and surge and go and come

And whisper, washing sucking sand away. ...

Or if I can I'll stay on land,

Run to lie in dead gray grass,

Not to fly:

Stick feathers in my hair.

Make songs. Make peace. Make truth with lies.

Make moments that will never.

That will never ever ever be.

Never. Ever.

Ever. Ever.

Be.

I didn't get to read the whole thing, though. Just two verses. Then the drums took over, loud in my ears— the drums that no one else could hear. The dreaming blindness filled my eyes awake. I lost sight of the words I had written. and there. instead. in front of me, was the image of the beach. The marsh, the low hummocks, the flat sand Marian had photographed for me so we would not forget. The subject of my recitation. Which now was drownded out by pounding that soon resolved to a spattering of applause.

The vision trickled away and left me stranded, scared. Why wasn't I asleep like all the times it happened before? I stumbled offstage. Leo was still clapping. I stormed past him, fear instantly transformed to rage. Shoved the door aside and stomped out to the street.

It was only 18 blocks. I began the walk home. Leo came out of the Cedar, calling my name, and I ignored him. His long legs caught me up, though, and that's when we had our fight.

It's stupid arguin against a drunk—they don't remember half what they say from one minute to the next, less than that of what you say no matter how many times you yell the same thing. Did no good but to pass the time.

By 2, when we had reached Paradise Alley, Leo seemed almost sober. So, at his insistence, I let him in. Less loud that way. He wanted to kiss and make up. I didn't. Told him go on back to his precious *mère*. He produced a couple more sheets torn from my poor book like that would make me feel better, and explained how he wasn't stealin them—which thought hadn't even occurred to me—but only figurin out how they could be improved on.

Improved.

Somehow I got him outta there without wakin the whole building.

Think I'll stay home tonight.

September 14 1953   All around me life went on all weekend, scales of college students' singin lessons, smells of fryin garlic, splash and suds and soapy scent of fresh laundry, but I was hiding. Hungry but I couldn't go out. He might find me. I had coffee. Sugar.

I had barely begun that book. Not much was in it
before it got lost. Taken. Six poems and the start of a
story with no idea how to end it. I'll be savin what I can.

This poem came from his pocket:

Four is round is compass white

Is challenging the starstruck night:

A tower owning all direction all potential

All the wreckless future past and time to either side

Where we may never someday go.

Oh no?

Oh yes:

We spin

We bless and wrench the windows open now

And crowd through making narrow wide

We are the fortune

We're the tide of moons

And we ignore the door

We four.

This one, too:

High above her shadow

Spilled like grease upon the island snow

A crow

Hopping the hedge of her hair

Such twigs of limbs so thin her legs so bent her arms

And crazy elbow angles;

But polish this blackness till she's sleek:

Her darkness shines

Alight.

My sister.

September 15 1953   Three poems recovered. Four, if you count the one he never even brought me but recited and I wrote it down. Though that was just part. Three-and-a-half. I still need the rest of that one and two more. And the start of that story. I don't care about whatever else I wrote.

If I can get it together enough to go out, I'll talk to Terry and ask him for his help. If I can't, I'll send him a letter.

I have to go out. I'm supposed to show up to work tomorrow.

September 16 1953   Nobody at the agency suspects a thing about me. Woke early due to another of those dreams. When Mr. Bright got in to open up the office I was already at my desk typing. Well, it was my plea to Terry, but musta looked good from where he stood. And I had the drafts and mock-ups set out in the order he likes; carried the first file in with his fresh cream and Danish.

Kept at it all morning like that, and he let me out for lunch in time to catch Marian in the Pulitzer's lobby.

She had brought a ham sandwich. We sat in the park and split it. I told her my woes. We took turns taking bites from an apple while she more or less said, "Tough titty." She has never held with mixin with whites—with any other races, really, despite our daddy bein Indian. "Just keep on," she said. "Do what you can with what you got. Recover whatever's missin. You remember anything you wrote?"

Only what the story was about—the coming of Clarice. And the ideas of the poems—but what good is half of heaven? More like a quarter ... each word, each syllable, so hard-won, the battle between sentence and abyss so hard-fought and now so lost. ...

September 17 1953   Busy imaginin how the magazine we were plannin is over before it's begun, it was a while till I became conscious of the bangin on my front door. The noise had been goin on a while. I didn't want to answer, but it only stopped to start up again a second later. Finally, I went to unlock and open up, and there stood this strange blond boy scowling down at me in clean clothes that were all torn and ragged and old. "Adam sent me," he said, and he stuck out his hand. "My name's Rafael." And he did sorta resemble an angel. A rude one livin like a hobo. I figured he must be another of Adam's little protégés. Sometimes he stashed em with me if not convenient for them to stay in his apartment.

"Come on in," I told him, and I fixed him a bed on the divan. Showed him the toilet and the key to the bathroom back along the floor's hallway. He nodded at everything and opened up his duffle to pull out a string bag of grapefruits. I accepted the one he offered. Payday ain't till tomorrow. Pension'll arrive in my mailbox in two more weeks.

I went in the kitchen for a knife and he came with me, but he peeled his grapefruit like an orange. Brought his duffle and dug around in it and this time came up with a notebook with the same covers as mine. But I knew it wasn't mine by the wear, plus when he opened it the pages were full of his writing. Matched what he was entering. I let him scribble a minute, then asked what the book was.

"An experiment," he called it. Another scowl, but this one seemed like it meant different things than the one at my door—more love? light? "I wanna shift rhythms like I'm playin, you know? Scattin." And I <u>did</u> know, and we talked about how to move emphasis and stretch syllables and similar poetry tricks such as the one I'm using now to show how our conversation just went on and on and on. He had some tea, too; we smoked that and talked more, and I damn near forgot about gettin up early to beat Mr. Bright in.

I shouldn'ta been over Leo this soon, but I found myself wishin as I watched Rafael settle his curly head on the spare pillow that he wasn't one of Adam's and we could try some experiments of our own.

Instead of which, I merely record the thought for posterity.

September 18 1953   Got home from depositin my check and buyin groceries to find a vase of flowers waitin outside my door. At first I admit I thought they were from Rafael. Thanks for puttin him up or something. Sunflowers and tiger lilies and a dark red dahlia in the center. I was examining the card when he walked up. Not his, he says—they were Leo's.

I oughta known Rafael wouldn'ta had the bread.

Inside I offered him salami on a roll. He ate it but didn't wanna wait around for me to cook a real supper since he was meetin Adam and Terry in an hour about getting a grant. He had come by to make sure I would let him sleep here again tonight. I said fine. Hardly got the door closed behind him leavin when I had to open it again to let in Leo.

The bouquet card had said he was sorry. He repeated the sentiment. I nodded that I understood and said "OK" to show I accepted his apology. I went in the kitchen to finish putting the food away and he followed me. "Sit on down," I told him, and waved at the stool by the table, but he shook his head and started pacin, lookin nervous.

Finally, I turned round from puttin the lettuce in the icebox and set my hands on my hips. "You got somethin more to say?" I asked, hopin I sounded as self-contained as Mama always did when she needed to figure out what rules we girls broke.

The man fell down on his knees! Was he hurt, I wondered? Then I saw the velvet jeweler box he was bringin outta his pants pocket, and oh the dread that filled me—was this gonna be a marriage proposal? Despite his assertion to not be of that mind? Because I ain't genuinely known Leo more than a couple weeks, though I've seen him hangin out a month or so longer.

But no. He gave me the box without a word, and I had to try four times to open it, but thank you jesus it was a necklace inside and not a ring. I started cryin from relief.

No doubt he misunderstood my feelings because he pitched into a mess of explanations about how important the pendant was to the history of his family, and it belonged to his mama's great-great-aunt and signified—I didn't exactly catch it, somethin about the

Spirit of France, resistance counter the Nazis. Obviously, he worried I was insulted because this pendant, this cross hangin from a chain, not only was it <u>not</u> a ring, it had no diamonds or rubies or pearls or emeralds encrusted on it, and it sure wasn't gold. Maybe silver. Platinum? Black inset was what—jet? Ebony?

While one part of my brain got practical about monetary value, the other part, the biggest part, was purely and simply stunned. The shape of that cross—I recognized it from ... somewhere. One of those damn dreams, maybe. After probably a minute starin down at it, I reached and took the box away from Leo's hand and he stopped talkin. He teetered a little standin up. I noticed, but I kept focused on the cross, pulling it loose, dragging its chain free and setting the box on the table, I guess. ...

Leo went behind me and helped me with the clasp. I traced along the cross's edges with my fingertips. "You really like it?" he asked me. His voice was wrong for a man who just gave a woman flowers and heirloom jewelry. Nervous as ever. The cool metal on my chest warmed with time and blood. I made him meet my eyes.

"What did you do?" I asked him.

He didn't want to say. Was it about my book, I asked him?

Yes, of course, it was.

He had sent a part of it to his publisher. Typed out the pages of my story and added his own ending. A collaboration, he called it. Stuck it in an envelope and put on stamps and mailed it off.

My story.

Gone.

I was mad. I grabbed at the cross and pulled till the chain cut my neck. It wouldn't break. Knocked the flowers off the drainboard, and their vase crashed in pieces in the sink. And then I thought, "Why am I wrecking my own stuff?"

My quiet, sensible self took charge. I quit yellin— hadn't realized that was what I was doing—and sat down on the chair. Leo crouched in front of me. He's brave, I'll give him that. He gathered my hands together and held them in his.

"You want me to say I'm sorry again?" he asked me. "I gotta tell you the truth. I'm not." He proceeded to lay it on me how what he'd done was for the best, I'd never make it on my own, I had a spark, special talent, but a colored like me wasn't gonna, had no chance of, would try and try and try again and always always fail to succeed.

I suppose he's right. It's for the best. This way I'll at least get some attention.

I wish I didn't care. I wish I could sleep.

September 19 1953   Rafael is missing. Last night I was glad he didn't come back here; with Leo staying it was a lot easier. Tonight, though, when we went by on the way to the Cedar, Adam acted surprised he wasn't with us. He said Rafael left their meeting to spend the night again on my couch.

Which, of course, was news to Leo. I acted like it was nothin big.

We all agreed we'd surely meet him at the bar. But he never showed, and I overheard Carmody and Roy bettin which jail he'd wound up in and for how long: county, federal, twenty-four hours courtesy the city. Could be.

Around closing, Leo wanted to go "home." My place. I needn'ta worried he would ask too many questions about Rafael; between the Cedar's whisky and the tequila bottle that he made the cabbie detour so he could buy he barely made it to bed. Me next.

September 20 1953   Leo only lives here Friday, Saturday, and Sunday. When he got up—hours after I did—my bathroom's frosted windows translucent with afternoon— his breath stank and his beard stubble rasprasprasped to the rhythm of his aggravated scratch. I ran him a tub and juiced him oranges and brewed him his coffee.

He said thanks and cleaned up but didn't touch the cup or glass. Then announced he had to talk to me. I pointed out how he was already talking. Seriously, he said he meant.

He wanted a schedule. He had to write, and everything was all set up at his mother's to accommodate his needs for doing that. I got how he wanted me to be fine with him spending weeknights away from me. We arranged things to his liking, which made him rub his forehead and wrinkle it like this had been too easy. Well, he ain't the only one has work to do.

Now the coffee was cold he asked for some. I cheated and warmed it up in a saucepan. Sitting out in the front room he didn't notice. He offered to take me to dinner, but I could see he was still not feelin a hundred per cent so I declined. Besides, I had just bought all them groceries and I hate for food to spoil.

I put water on to boil for pasta and chopped some onions and he left—probably worried he wouldn't be able to stand the smell of them cooking. I made spaghetti and sauce—extra in case Rafael returned. So far, he hasn't.

September 21 1953   According to our schedule, Leo and I will see each other at Adam's Wednesday night but not come here afterwards. Since this week I'm only due in the office Thursday and Friday that's cool by me. Now I know what's up with my missing story I can get going on new work. Like this:

Down
on the
Farm

Wanda hated chickens, but she had to live with them. Gramma Jerry just loved those big old ugly birds. She let them in the house. She said they ate the bugs. Wanda was only little, and she couldn't explain why exactly having chickens in your house was wrong. But she knew it was wrong for certain and for sure.

Gramma Jerry lived on a farm. To visit the nearest neighbor meant driving her truck along bumpy brown roads. It was far and they didn't go over other people's houses often. But when they did, Wanda noticed one thing: no chickens inside.

One day they came back from a nice visit. The family Wanda and Gramma Jerry visited, the Clarks, had given them cake and lemonade to eat and bring home. Gramma Jerry took the heavy, cold, slippery jar of lemonade in herself and let Wanda carry in the box of cake. Wanda was so proud! She walked up the steps without tripping, without even the tiniest stumble, and Gramma Jerry held open the screen door.

But before she could climb the stool to set the cake box on the kitchen counter, WHAM! She was on her butt on the linoleum! That mean, rusty-colored hen called Ruby went and knocked her down! Then Ruby's sharp beak sliced right through the cardboard box and slashed the cake into pieces. Stabstabstab! Cake and frosting exploded in the air like sugar fireworks, and Wanda exploded in tears and screams.

"Waaaah!" Instead of scaring Ruby off, Wanda's crying brought the other chickens on the run, the whole flock clucking and sticking their heads forward every stupid step. All around her! Wanda made fists and waved her arms around like a pinwheel, hitting Ruby and the other hens like they were fluffy dandelions. They squawked and backed under the kitchen table to blink at her with beady eyes.

Wanda sat by herself in a big mess of crumbs and feathers and smears of frosting. And silence.

Then a huge roar of laughter filled the room! The house! It spilled all over the yard—Gramma Jerry was laughing! Laughing out loud! The chickens looked upset by the noise— and suddenly that was funny! They were funny! All huddled under the table and chairs and peeking from beneath like it was raining, like every laugh was a raindrop from the sky of Gramma Jerry's joyful heart.

Wanda laughed, too. Gramma Jerry picked her up and kissed her. "Never you mind about cleaning that up now, baby girl. Come on and wash your hands and change your clothes and leave them hens to finish what they begun."

Wanda took a long cool bath and put on her pajamas and got in bed. Gramma Jerry served them both bowls of ice cream. She told jokes Grampa Perry used to tell. They laughed till Wanda's stomach muscles got too sore.

When they were done she felt tired and dreamy. Ruby poked her head around the corner. Wanda just smiled. "Silly chickens," she whispered to herself and Gramma Jerry. And then she fell asleep.

September 22 1953   That was weird. Think I wrote a kids' book. Needs some work—the heroine solves a problem no one had. I can fix that, though, change the names, maybe see how to get it published.

Yeah, it's kinda cool. And not at all the sorta thing Leo's gonna claim as his own.

Also, I found Rafael today. I got tired of not knowin where he was. Went over to Marian's office to use the phone. Put on my best white lady voice and called a bunch of likely jails. No sign. Then I tried the hospitals. Took all afternoon. Finally turned him up way off at Creedsmoor in Queens. He had committed himself for the weekend to get clean—then they wouldn't let him go without somewhere official and permanent to stay. So tomorrow I am going to collect him and bring him back here. Somehow.

September 23 1953   So hard. I didn't have money for a 15-mile cab ride—30, round trip. I took the F train, which took over an hour. Dressed up in Marian's cutdown best suit, the shantung silk with the matching pillbox hat, I walked all the way to Creedsmore from the station—more like sauntered, because I didn't wanna get all hot and sweaty and smelly.

Unlike what I expected, the nurse at reception gave me hardly any trouble. No, that was up to the doctor on the ward. I was prepared, though—rent receipts and utility bills in my purse, which he had the nerve to look at. And I could tell he thought me and Rafael were screwin and he hated the idea. I wondered what kinda story I oughta tell him to convince him otherwise—would he believe Rafael to be colored, a relation tryin to pass? I opened my mouth, but the lie wouldn't come out. So I sat where the doctor left me, in a stuffy little waiting room with no windows, long enough I began to think he was lockin <u>me</u> up steada releasing Rafael to my care.

But at last, at last a set of steps out of all those that had been passing by slowed down and stopped. The metal door opened to reveal an orderly with a hairy hand clamped onto Rafael's thin shoulder. Do angels ever get sick and pale? Do they show bruises on the skin beneath their blue eyes? Rafael clutched his coat and duffel like they were his hope of glory and smiled like the sun goin in and out of wind-whipped clouds: bright but flickerin.

"Sis! I knew you'd come!"

So now I had to support this totally spurious claim. "You little scalawag!" I said in Miss-Anne mode. "Mother and Father will be furious!" The doctor hovered outside the still-open door. I made sure he could hear. Let him puzzle it out.

I walked out of the hospital entrance with Rafael leaning half his weight on our interlaced arms. We took a taxi; I had already planned on riding to the train station, but Rafael looked so weedy I decided to spend money I didn't really have the right to spend to take us all the way.

There was spaghetti sittin in the icebox left over from Sunday, but Rafael wasn't up for eating that. He swallowed down some apple cider I heated with cinnamon sticks, and I laid him out on the divan again, nappin like a new kitten. Now to get washed and ready for me and Leo's date.

I don't have time to write much about our fight. This the second. Leo never sticks to a plan, not even one he drew up himself, so of course he came here when we were supposed to meet at Adam's and stormed out jealous at the sight of Rafael innocent and asleep. We made up.

But then—that's what matters the most. Then. That's what I need to concentrate on explaining.

I guess I'll call it another dream. But I was awake. I know.

I chased Leo out to the sidewalk and made him sit with me in the courtyard to talk. Mostly, I listened to him tell me why he acted so asinine. We ended with me apologizing and assuring him Rafael was just a kid, nothin to me, very likely a fairy and no threat, no threat at all. Prove it, Leo said. He wanted me to kick him out.

Well, of course I couldn't do that, but I assumed I better not say so. At a loss, I asked Leo to wait a minute, then crept up, and slid Rafael's duffel from behind the sofa where he'd stashed it and lugged it back down. I told Leo I was takin it to Adam's, and when we returned its owner would be gone.

I have smoked that much tea a dozen times. Drugs weren't the cause.

This is the autumn equinox. So? There's one of those each and every year. I simply do not understand why I

When it first started I felt as if I was goin outside. But at the same time I was on Adam's floor in a circle with everybody else: Leo with his head on my lap again, Roy and Annie, Terry, Carmody, Adam, Frankie, Camille, that Julian who sometimes comes around—all of us. I wasn't goin anywhere. Besides, what am I tryna say? Outside what? The room, the apartment? The world?

Stillness hung all around me, like snow at midnight. And quiet—I heard Blakey on the record player, heard what Roy was sayin about why women aren't jazz musicians, heard Annie's slightly shamed laugh, but through a shut window, it seemed. The music was elsewhere, hardly in my ears at all. I put my hand out and like I was <u>pushing</u>, like the air was <u>solid</u>, I moved that slow! I think I made some sound, a grunt—couldn't for once come up with words—Leo musta heard me, and he turned his head with the speed of a redwood in a growth spurt, puckered his lips—a joke, but I couldn't kiss him; it would take forever.

Took almost as long to stand and go to the window. Centuries I wrestled it open. At last, the sharp air, dark and clean, blew in my face. Through that cold—which did not wake me or shake me or quicken time—I saw me. Not a reflection. Me, nine years old.

I saw me looking up. Not from the street nor the sidewalk—the ground where this girl-me stood was the old garden in the shadow of our house on Ridge Avenue.

Poor little child, bit by mosquitoes and bedbugs, thin-legged and hopin for more from life: beauty. Meaning. Things I realized I had now, makin friends with all these artist types. "Marlene!" I called. "Sweet Marlene—I remember!" I did, like the night was full of yesterday. Yesteryear. To encourage her to listen I leaned forward into the black light. "You can do it—you will! You're gonna—" A knock on the door behind me. I turned and saw Adam already answering it—the jello atmosphere had dissolved without me noticing and he opened it normally—everything was normal—and there stood Rafael. He crooked a finger, and Adam tilted his head down to catch what he whispered, then frowned in my direction.

"You better come here," said Adam.

"Okay." I looked out the window at myself one last time. Didn't want to leave me, but too much noise outta Adam and the others would notice. I was hopin they wouldn't. Leo, especially—I scrambled fast as I could out onto the landing. "In a minute," I told Adam and stepped out and pulled shut his apartment door and dragged Rafael up the stairs to these nice shadows one floor up.

"I got your stuff down there. It's safe," I said.

"I know," he said back, and went on how he wasn't worried about that. Somethin else. Me.

He said he was in love with me.

I swear I only reached out to pat him "too bad" on his shoulder. So it's a mystery how we wound up wound around each other in a hug so tight we might as well have sunk inside each other's skin. And oh my, that kiss. I fought gravity or somethin stronger and ended it. Just in time to lean over the railing and see Leo's face vanish from the cracked open door to Adam's.

He looked awful. Like a wall covered in dirty white paint. Dirty and peelin.

"How about that." Rafael wasn't askin.

I never wanted to hurt anyone. Not that bad. "Maybe we better leave for a while," I suggested. Rafael nodded and we climbed down the stairs to the entry and left out to the sidewalk. No sign there of the garden or our old house or little me.

We walked slow. The hour passed from deep night to almost dawn. Mist swirled up outta nowhere. Under a streetlamp I noticed it laid tiny spangles on my angel's hair. On his long lashes.

We had been walkin apart, but I stopped then in appreciation. He unfurled his hand like a flower under water and held it out for me to take without the least doubt I would. The most gorgeous thing I ever saw.

We continued on. Eventually, we reached my building. I had my keys. But I didn't want to go in—not really; that would end our walk. Which you'd think I wanted to do. End it in bed. I mean, isn't the point of everything? To fuck?

No, it's not. The point is to make it, and by make it, I mean mesh: minds, bodies, pasts, futures, fears, hopes, dreams.

I also wanted to stay outside in case Leo came, and then I could claim innocence and tell him he was wrong about what he witnessed. And I wanted to be wrong myself about what I done. Mostly, though, I simply wanted to walk forever and for always beside my angel.

But what did he want?

The courtyard's tallest tree swayed in the first breeze of the morning. The mist tore to pieces and the temp dropped while the sky turned silver. Rafael was shiverin in his holey sweater—I had left his jacket packed in the duffle back at Adam's. So I took him in after all. He was my responsibility.

Inside the warmth, we kissed some more. No hurry. We lay down on the covers on the divan. Melted together.

Our stomachs started talkin to each other. I laughed, got up, made us eggs and toast. Rafael got up, too, and made us this special Indian tea—not American Indian like Daddy, India Indian. He used pepper and cinnamon and cloves, and there were supposed to be other spices he didn't have because guess where they were?

On the walk we hadn't talked, but now as we ate we did. And after. I left late for work. Before I went I told him all about the thing that happened before he got to Adam's. He didn't straight out call me crazy, which is comforting, considering he would know by comparison. Considering where he's been all weekend. I got the idea he was familiar with a similar phenomenon. Because he asked smart questions, like was this the first time I had this kinda dream while I was awake?

That question was when I realized. No. How could I have forgotten? The first time was at the Cedar on the stage. Only eleven days ago.

September 24 1953   Mr. Bright seemed actually kinda relieved when I barely scooted into the office on time. Wasn't much to do there these couple of days anyway: I opened letters from the magazine's readers, sorted through pitches for articles and illustrations we probably wouldn't use, made sure he saw a request for free back issues from a grade school. Low priority correspondence which the boss dictated answers for with a marked lack of verve. I didn't request it but he waved me out for lunch early and I met Marian in her office before she even had her scarf tied. We got to the hot dog cart ahead of almost everybody and didn't have to wait long to be served. "My treat," I told Marian, and she accepted the favor, probably since it was so cheap.

The wind picked up and chilled us a little despite the sun. We began walking around the park's edge to circulate our blood. But when I gave her my story to read Marian ducked behind the shelter of Horace Greeley's statue and stood still a while. I couldn't tell by lookin at her blank expression what she thought. I figured she was done when she grunted and shut my book. "Yeah, that could work," she said, and she grunted again.

"You have an idea?" I asked her. I was hoping. Marian knows far more about publishing than I do, because besides magazines, she has worked in book companies, too—Alfred A. Knopf, for instance, which is a major one.

"I'm thinkin Little, Brown might be interested," she said. She named a few more places to send it to if they aren't.

"Of course, it's way too long. And you need a good artist." I had thought it was too short. "Someone who's okay using only one or two colors."

We went inside so she could cross out extraneous words. If there were gonna be drawings and paintings, no need to describe so much. Then I rode the elevator to the office where I normally work and pretended to earn my pay. Really I was retypin my book—a worse crime than when I wrote my letter to Terry on the clock. According to Marian, it needs a new title, so I'm just callin it my book for now.

Mr. Bright went home around four. I called Marian on his phone, and she came up and read my new version. She says it's better. Even though I added how Gramma Jerry was sad and cryin over Grampa Perry's death, which was why laughin at the chickens is a happy ending? It is shorter, too.

I made double copies and gave my sister one. Tomorrow I'll write a letter to go with the final draft with the right title and mail it out. And that will get my career in motion.

When I left my apartment this morning I gave Rafael the extra key. My trust was rewarded. Deliciousness wafted out of the window as I walked home from the corner. I shouted hello as I unlocked the front door and came in. Piled high with sheets and pillows and blankets, the divan was the same mess. I heard him answer back from the kitchen, which was worse—but filled with the smell of the reason why. The man had made meatloaf— the oven hung open to show it glistenin brown—and mashed potatoes, with what looked like a nice smooth gravy bubblin on the stove top. And he was stirrin a pan of string beans, too, grinnin up at me, cheeks rosy from the heat.

"Come here," I told him, and he set the spoon down and came.

I think I am in love.

September 25 1953   Picked up a bit at the office today, which is good. An author sent a story early, and Mr. Bright let me take a stab at proofing it. I know all the marks from seeing his. I addressed the back issues for that school and then impressed him by taking them down to be mailed myself. No need for Mr. Bright to know I slipped my manuscript out with them.

Nobody home when I got here, but Rafael had left a note in an envelope. I poured myself a glass of milk and drank it with a leftover piece of the pie he baked last night, then opened it.

I saved what he wrote me under my pillow, so I don't have to copy the whole thing here. Sweet but troublin. Sometimes you get caught up in complications that don't actually make a difference to anyone else. He better let me worry about Leo.

I did check. His bag is gone.

□

I'm so very sorry. I said it over and over. I'm sorry sorry sorry sorry sorry.

I really should have expected him. I went to Adam's thinking stupidly that would be where Rafael was staying. I had completely forgotten Leo was supposed to meet me there. Adam opened the door, but not wide enough I could come in. Kept the chain on, but soon as I said hello how are you, Leo's face appeared over his shoulder. His eyes had grown bigger or his face shrunk. I dunno. He shoved Adam aside and shut the door—but I heard the chain slide and he opened it right back up and grabbed my arm and hauled me inside. Adam huffed out a little laugh, but seemed fine with what amounted to taking over his place. <u>His</u> place.

Leo ignored my questions about Rafael and hustled me past people lounging in the living room to the kitchen. My angel was nowhere to be seen on the way. He let go of me but blocked the door. So big.

"You," he said. Just that one word. He shut his eyes, and it shocked me to see tears squeezing out. "You can't." He opened them and lunged toward me and I balled my fists up fast—I'd punch him in the nose! I'd kick his shins! I'd bite! I'd scream his ears off!

Only he dived for my knees and hugged them and buried his head in my crotch, howlin and sobbin full throttle. I had no defense against that. Took all the fight outta me.

Then the sound of him crying went from muffled to whisper soft. Slow as sadness. A faraway lullabye. My raised arms and my fists uncurling to claws drifted steada dropped in air thick as Karo syrup. The papered walls wafted out away from us replaced by this vague notness, and the ceiling—I raised my eyes and it was gone, too, notness obscured by clouds of no color coming to wrap us around and the floor, too—it was all vanished.

Leo peeped up from my bluejeans. His face changed from grief to fear to wonder. "Marlene?" he said. "What's going on?" The sobbing song went on in the background. Above it, his voice sounded the same as ever—a little high maybe. He pulled himself up to stand towering over me. "Where's Adam's?" His hands clutched tight at my shoulders.

Probably the point was more where were we. I shifted so I could look where Leo was lookin. Seemed I saw a shining—like the sun comin out—but dimmer than that—like a movie screen? Here's what was showin: me and Leo, older, with three kids, sittin at a picnic table.

Everyone except me looked happy.

I—went away—from that. I wouldn't say I walked. Just wanted to get farther off, so I did. The echoes of Leo's sobbing song faded away till I could hear whispers of other music—sweeter, like it was played through a honeycomb. At the same time, a few more shining spots appeared in the mist, and I went toward the nearest one. Whether I meant to or not, I left Leo behind. In the next clear patch, a gold-leaved willow drooped branches over my sleeping angel. Light from a day beyond glinted on his soft-sprouting beard. Which was too long to have grown that fast since yesterday, wasn't it? I reached to find out for sure but could not break into this bubble afternoon.

Another, larger patch spread from my attempts and lapped back to cover that amber glow with a pale fire like mother-of-pearl. In this scene Rafael awake chanted something making hardly any sound—I saw his mouth moving, his breathing rise and fall, his curl-covered head nod in time to those nearly silent beats. The window I saw him in expanded to the size of a door, revealing his night, his stars, puddles of rain reflecting a black and silver sky. Revealing me, too, apparently, to him—our eyes met. My Rafael smiled even as he kept saying whatever chant or song or poem was being said. He gestured me toward him with cupped hands. I could almost hear his words. I leaned forward and took one step across the falling barrier—and got yanked back. A big hard hand on my elbow pulled me around to face Leo. "Stop!" he told me. And again, "You can't."

I was pretty sure I could. I would duck under his arms and jump the hoop and be with Rafael. Wherever he was. I twisted loose, but Leo caught me two-handed this time. His face looked savage. "You can't throw yourself away on that <u>bum</u>!"

At last, a whole sentence. I liked it. I'm colored but Rafael isn't good enough for me? Wait till Marian hears.

"He's been in jail," Leo went on. "He's a hustler and a queer. Never held a job—"

No more half-heard words. Only a kind of buzzing, bare and soft and deep. The door was a window, a single pane. I fought like an orangutan, but Leo held onto me. The soft buzz dropped off to nothing. The size of the opening shrunk to an eye and winked out.

So did all the other openings. Then the notness thinned, and behind it was the return of the kitchen: linoleum floor, Martian red formica, and mustard yellow painted cabinets, walls, and ceiling. Adam shut the door to the bathroom and turned to frown at us. He just knew we weren't there the moment before, he said. He asked Leo to go get "the letter," then told me he'd sent Rafael to Terry's for safekeeping. To keep him safe, he means, from Leo punching him in the head. The famous author was jealous of a "bum."

The letter was from Terry, an apology for taking and sharing and then, he said, losing my book. No explanation how. Saying he's to blame.

I guess I better be glad Leo stole what he did. All that's left of it.

September 26 1953   Leo continues to believe he owns my weekends. I do love him. Not the same, but for real.

His plan for today is that Roy will drive us to Brighton Beach where Terry's aunt lets him use the family cottage after Labor Day. Of course, Rafael's there, and of course, I don't want to see the two of them in a knockdown— one's strong, one's sneaky, and neither deserves what's probably coming to em.

So I gotta get sick.

September 27 1953   Leo's bein really good to me. And Adam let him use his phone to call Marian, who had to ask me why I ate half a jar of peanut butter when I know oily food upsets my stomach so. Leo found that reassuring, that I've felt this way before. He'll go back to his mère's tonight.

September 28 1953   I let Marian make me an appointment with her doctor. Not because I threw up and couldn't eat for twenty-four hours. Not that kind of doctor. He's the one she's been seein about the alcohol. She thinks Dee can help with the mess I've created with Rafael and Leo. So I'm showin up at his office tomorrow.

Tomorrow is Rafael's Saint Day.

September 29 1953   I have a tiny bit of homesickness for Brooklyn from when as a child I would visit Marian there, and of course, from when later I came there to stay. Dee's office is basically the ground floor of the house he lives in—which is why no suite numbers—on a cul-de-sac up against the cemetery. On my way this afternoon I walked past a few of the same vintage in poorer condition, and one even appeared abandoned—but not in a dangerous way. I got that feeling of—of land reclaiming human vacancy, ailanthus trees and walnuts and wild birds left over from some moment before we began telling time—I dunno how to describe this exactly, but when I rang the buzzer under Dr. Dee's sign I felt the sadness of these elements as they came back into their own ... like a muscle appreciative of its own soreness ... I will work on saying this more clearly. For now I'll stick to writing what I can, how I can. The house is brick and wood painted green with white trim and has a wide porch with cement stairs, not a stoop. When I got there I noticed curtains covered all the windows, including the one runnin the length of the door. A bland-looking white man wearing his hair long ushered me into an empty waiting room and turned out to be the doctor himself, per his handshake and introduction. He went to a desk and asked me questions to fill out a form and start a file on me and suddenly the way he was sittin and typin I wasn't sure anymore I was talkin to a man. I've decided to go with my gut for now.

File took next to no time. Soon we wound up in a second room with quiet walls. There was some kind of pattern on them that matched the movement of the overture just beginning, white on whiter white—

"Whoa there!" said Dr. Dee. He stretched a hand toward my belly like he was catching a kid from falling off a train seat when the brakes hit hard. "This is as good a place as any for heading 'outside'—better than most, in fact, which is not a coincidence—but your sister tells me you have Issues." He pronounced the quote marks and the capital "I". "Let's deal with those before getting into more serious teachings." Which he said he could tell I had a talent that needed his guidance. But not right now.

So I filled him in on Rafael and Leo. More than filled him in—I kinda spilled over the brim of the basic info necessary and said what I really wanted from them, what was potential as well as actual ... Leo's words blending with mine, his soft lips, the tender back of Rafael's neck, the daring in his low-lidded eyes, so forth, so on.

When I ended and we finally sat in silence—me sunk in a low armchair, Dr. Dee leaning forward in its twin—I waited in vain for his help resolving my dilemma. Instead, he challenged me to explain <u>why</u> I had to make a choice. I brought up Leo's jealousy. "That is someone else's emotion," Dee replied. "Not yours. And it's nobody's reason."

Why do I believe I have to pick one man over the other? I'm supposed to write an answer and bring it back to him in a week. Homework.

That's not all. I have a book to read by then. Almost a journal like mine: a copy of a very local history his great-great-great Aunt Elvira Coker wrote called <u>The Three Rivers</u>. It's about how the New Bedford Rose first bloomed. He thinks its philosophy will help me.

It's better. This doctor of Marian's is charging me $25 a session. Good thing Daddy's pension check comes tomorrow. I'm not even on any medicine yet. That is probably gonna cost even more.

Sometimes I wonder would Daddy care for what I'm doin with his money. Especially since he always used to talk about the importance of "getting an education."

I already have one, thank you, and I'm able to counter my gloomy doubts with this thought: being with most whites is a truly educational experience.

Glow

September 29 1963 It musta been him. Over eight years since the last time I saw him, but that's my angel. Silver in his golden hair—I think? I gotta go back and make sure. But can I? South Beach Hospital has separate wings for men and women, and visitin Clarice there a second time will only take me in the one and not the other. Not the wing where they would be keepin him.

I was in my sister's wing. Five floors up. Barred window in the way. Yet, I swear.

Maybe because I had him on my mind because today was his Saint's Day, which I have always, always remembered. But no, I wasn't really thinkin about Rafael that moment but about Clarice and why she wound up in that brandstinkingnew firetrap of a building. How Mama decided she couldn't care for her anymore and barely let me know she had committed her to the state. Her own daughter. I guess since the relationship ain't blood Mama don't believe it matters all that much.

And if I hear her right, pretty soon she'll wanna do worse.

September 30 1963   Mama was absolutely correct about one thing: no way she could take care of Clarice. This mornin I went by her room bringin groceries. She didn't even bother pretending she was gettin outta bed. "Just sit the bag over there, Marlene," she says, waving a hand at the stand with the radio on it like she don't care. Like she don't need anything. I didn't talk back, but I unpacked the cream and put that in her little camping cooler. There were some papers stickin out from under the radio, and when I looked at them closer, I realized what they were about: electroshock treatment for my sister. But Mama hadn't signed them yet, and I smuggled them out under my sweater. Maybe she'll forget. For a while at least.

Caught a cab back home. Julian's still in London, or somewhere north of there, Oxford or some shit. Rattled around the place like my jewelry in that box he gave me on our wedding anniversary. Plenty of room. Mama coulda stayed here if she wasn't so stubborn. Marian, too. Imagine them in the same apartment, though.

I'll ask Dr. Dee what to do about Clarice. I'm <u>so</u> glad Julian insisted on me seeing somebody and he agreed to pay what I owed for me to go back to Dee. Maybe Julian can help with my problems with my sisters. One or both of em. Money.

Planning to ask my husband for a favor when he gets home had me feelin nervous. I messed around a while in my office, rearranging a few reference files and rereading some letters I used writing the latest book, the one about being a Beat.

Found my ten year-old "homework" where I wrote why I thought I had to choose between goin with Leo or Rafael. Boils down to violence: I was scared of gettin my head knocked in. By guess which one? It's a good reminder.

Also found a pocket-size sketchpad full of Roses, with my first diagram labeling the Five Petals the way Dr. Dee taught me: Thought, Action, Observation, Integration, New Action. The basics. Glad I had the Three Rivers book after I had to quit so I could keep up my practice; in addition to improving my control over my trips "outside," using the New Bedford Rose helped me through those sad weeks right after my angel vanished. Still does, on occasion. But what finally calmed me down this time was opening up and holding onto and reading Rafael's last note. Again.

October 1 1963 You'd think being even a little famous would make this kinda thing easier. First off, the receptionist come all white on me sayin how the hospital's <u>public</u> visiting hours weren't till the afternoon and did I have a physician's license or proxy or something I of course had no hope in heaven of ever obtaining and I bet she wouldn't know if it bit her narrow behind. I smiled so hard and kept standin at her desk till she sent for her supervisor. Now <u>she</u> recognized my name. Or should I say Julian's name. Ushered me into a chair in her private office and poured me a cup of hot tea and let me look through their records.

No Rafael. Unless he's usin a new name, too.

Supervisor took me herself to where they had Clarice. Apologizing all the way, explaining how they were still "putting the finishing touches on the grounds" and flimflam of that sort. What did that have to do with tyin my sister to her bedframe?

Her long hair cut. I got my own cut and I get it permed, too, but it ain't Clarice without braids so long they wrap twice around her head. A crown.

She said hello, and to my eyes she looked completely lucid. That blue sack they called a dress wasn't exactly complimenting her complexion, but no drool, no fightin the restraints like Sunday. We reminisced a bit about bein kids together and about scattering Daddy's ashes off the ferry. I promised I'd come again soon. I meant it. Then I had the orderly escort me back to the supervisor's office who was sorry some more, but whether Claire stayed at South Beach wasn't in her control. Or mine. Mama is the closest kin, not me, and the electroshock is scheduled to start next week, soon as they have an opening.

October 2 1963   I'm in the habit now of writin in my journal. Every night and every day. Like it's automatic it's so easy.

I asked Dr. Dee about me seein Rafael, and he says I ain't crazy and there could be two ways of explainin what happened. Typical Freudian analysis: I displaced my anxiety over Clarice onto my environment and dredged up his disappearance as a stand-in for my real worry. True as far as it goes, I guess. But also Dee suggested maybe Rafael was really there.

I like that idea.

According to him, "outside" is a lot more accessible around South Beach and similar psychiatric institutions. So I coulda been hoverin between worlds, coulda caught a glimpse into Rafael's whereabouts, either in this one or that one—which is where I had suspected he went to hide when they charged him with that poor man's murder.

Regarding what next, Dee as before urged me to use the Rose. Okay, skipping the first two Petals? Because I had been Observing hard after Sunday to no avail. But when I told him that he shook his head. I'd got it wrong apparently. I was spozed to come up with a strategy for the Thought and then implement it for the Action.

Then Observe the results of <u>that</u>. Then Integrate my Observations.

He wasn't tellin me what to do, just reminding me how to figure out how to figure it out. And then the hour was up.

I made an extra appointment to see him again before Julian's back. Monday.

October 3 1963   One more week and one more day. Julian is going to be so proud! I haven't telephoned him since he left except to make sure he arrived safely. Wrote him, yeah. Not like constantly, though. Instead, I am focused on giving interviews. Which I have hated ever since I had to start doin them for my first picture book. I simply hate answering them same stupid questions over and over. I know it promotes the memoir, though, so I been saying yes every time the publisher wants me to do one.

This morning's wasn't so bad—it was for a radio station, but I didn't mind because the studio's in the opposite direction from Mama's, and getting ready and going in there kept my mind off her and Clarice. The reporter asked the same things they all ask: how many "beatniks" I slept with, which ones used the most drugs, and what was Leo like. Well, he's alive, how about you interview <u>him</u>, I said.

I mean, he's steady writing. Not exactly steady, but he had a book come out last year about his dead brother, and if he don't have another book this year, it ain't because they ain't clamorin for more. That's what Marian says.

October 4 1963   Speak of the Devil. Or write of him anyway. Picked up the receiver in the middle of the night last night and it wasn't bad news or my husband in England. Leo, drunk. His voice like a sad tenor sax. He wanted to see me. Why would I want to see him? For old time's sake, he kept mumbling. Then it hit me. My book. It's coming out next week.

I had the publisher send him a copy—well after he coulda made me change anything, but with plenty of time for him to say how good it is so they could quote him on the cover. Which he hasn't done but I could still use his help.

So I'm meeting him for lunch. I'll take him to that Chinese place on Fulton. Then I can go cry on Marian's shoulder afterwards since it's near her job, just a few blocks north of Hoyt. Even closer than when we first went.

Goddammit. What he wanted in return. He oughta know better. And then to bring up how much Julian and Rafael look alike? Was that supposed to convince me to go to bed with <u>him</u>? I was too mad to cry by the time the cab dropped me at Winslow & Hooper and Marian was out sick anyway. Wound up stomping down the avenue in a righteous fit. I walked twenty blocks before I could cool myself and get on with the rest of my day.

Mama was home, naturally. She never goes nowhere but church, and that's quite the production. What I didn't expect was finding Marian there. Her coat was buttoned, but I got her to wait to leave till I'd put dinner on Mama's tray and sliced the meat off the pork chop and into little strips.

We shared the first cab we could catch, which took a while in that neighborhood. While we were waiting I asked why she didn't go to work and she said she was headin for <u>The Ladder,</u> this bulldyke magazine she has started to help put out. One of those plain brown wrapper productions. I hope she doesn't get in trouble.

October 5 1963   Here is my Rose diagram for Clarice:

The first Petal's self-explanatory. Self-evident. Long legs and long straight hair and a laugh like beer or champagne bubbles. She <u>has</u> to be free or freedom makes no damn sense. That's my Thought.

The second Petal's where I run into problems. I go back and forth trying to decide what's the best Action. The least drastic? Like talkin Mama into takin her back home? Except there's no such a place. Not no more. So it may come down to me breaking her out.

The third Petal's easy again. Watch her. See how she does when I get her out, to where I call "over the fence." Or maybe I should bring her back on this side? Once we walk free of the hospital guards. ... Julian would understand if I asked for her to stay with us. But outside or not, no trick to it. I'm a writer. Observation's what I do.

Fourth Petal feels kinda vague. Necessarily, I guess. What am I gonna be Integrating into what? Things I learn from the third Petal into a new plan?

Because that's the fifth Petal, always. Bloom after bloom, garden without end. New Action.

Okay, I know. Always known. Fourth Petal is making the new plan once I see how things are with her. Fifth Petal is putting it to work.

What about Rafael? Dr. Dee told me I need to draw another Rose for him.

October 6 1963   Mama still insists on getting herself ready for church. Every week. God knows what time she has to wake up to hobble on them canes to the bathroom. But all I am supposed to do is drive up in the taxi and wait for her to come out.

Marian is not allowed to go with us. I mistakenly told Mama one time I was contemplatin Buddhism and nearly got banned alongside my sister as a heathen idolater. Nevermind the preachers say we're all sinners; some sins are worse than others apparently.

It's a mostly Negro congregation of a mostly white people's religion. All Souls Episcopal. Mama joined after Daddy died. They had the funeral service, so I don't know if the place was just familiar to her from that, or if something in the eulogy touched her heart. Most likely, though, is Esther is right when she figures since they took up a collection Mama feels beholden to them. Esther suggested that as the reason for the sudden conversion this spring. Then she laughed. Let her. She don't have to worry about Mama's increasing eccentricities except when she and her family visit from Wilmington for Mother's Day and Thanksgiving, and Christmas and Easter. Which may seem like it's a lot to her.

Episcopal is a lot like Catholic. Music's got good chords, no rhythm. Sermon's almost always a drag, a drone, a bore, a snore. Wouldn't want Mama jumpin up gettin happy anyway.

Skirts are de rigueur. And scarves. Women supposed to cover our heads like our hairstyles are nets to fish up men in. Traps.

Said it was like Catholics.

I had the cabbie stop for a nice chicken take-out for our dinner. Dawdle over that as much as I could, though,

111

plenty empty hours remained at the end of my ride home. Evening sky like blue velour outside the windows.

Empty hours.

I moped a short while, then decided to look for Rafael's Rose.

Found it a few minutes ago. Dug through a trunk of papers I had to sort out anyway, my more recent journals, and poems and starts to stories or who knows maybe novels. Jumbled in with that sketchpad and stuff—while I was putting together the book I dumped anything visibly not letters or other relevant memorabilia I had stored in there to deal with later. Later's now.

October 7 1963   Dr. Dee's worth every dollar I have Julian pay him. Includin the back fees. Today he surprised me by sayin both my ideas for getting Clarice out make sense but to also come up with one factoring in Rafael. Include a delusion as part of my plans? I asked. To which he replied that some delusions are real. Then he handed me Rafael's new poetry collection.

Well, I got it here now by my bed. First name's spelled a little different with a "ph" not "f" in the middle of it, and "Mason" changed to "Macon." But the photo of him on the back is one Annie took at Adam's the time he was staying there and we met. Sprawled out on the sofa, seemin so pleased with himself like he just invented God. Smoke in a dissipating halo. He didn't look that young in my hallucination last week.

In California it was only one o'clock, and they answered the phone at Open Books on the second ring. It took a while, but I was finally connected to the editor who bought Rafael's manuscript. He said it was very interesting how many people wanted to know how to get in touch with the author. Who else? I asked. His brother, which I didn't know he had a brother, but that's what the man said, and a reporter I recognized the name of who had interviewed me. I made three. Not really a lot, but as the editor put it, enough to be more than usual.

Venom Sweet has only been out a week. I know it's Rafael's work. Some lines I remember he showed me in his notebook. Back when I was a poet, too.

But what I do is also good. And the editor—Mr. Lucius Smallwood—when he realized who I was, he was so apologetic about not being able to help. The ms. came in unagented, "over the transom," and they mailed the contract and advance check and galley to a post office box.

I told him thanks and promised I'd come through the store if I ever went to San Francisco. Though I haven't heard nothin outta my publishers concernin a tour. Hung up.

It's a thin book. Ninety-some pages.

My Rose for Rafael is obsolete. But I knew that when I went to find it. I mean I made it when they charged him, before he disappeared. But I thought I could update it pretty easy if he was still gone. Now, probably not.

October 8 1963   I had the driver drop me off around Seaview and Magnolia so I could reconnoiter South Beach. Soon as the car pulled outta sight I "climbed the fence" like Dr. Dee had been coaching me to do and went "outside." Almost always misty there these days. Draws back sometimes, but it never completely clears. I have learned not to worry. Hold the Thought. Don't let the close-to-music distract me. I trained my mind on Clarice and found my way in. Didn't have to sneak, neither. I simply walked in past whoever was supposed to be on guard to her room. Say, her cell.

I had come before official visiting hours, and I saw the ugly truth. Clarice's hair was dirty with crusted-up vomit. Which, give them credit, a nurse was there with a wet comb and a bowl of water going through it and murmuring nice, soothing words. Clarice had her eyes closed at first, and it was like everything was fine and she'd just gone to a new hairdresser's. But she opened them and they were red with veins. When I saw that I saw other bad signs. Broken nails. Bruises on her wrists and arms and legs and ankles. On her neck. Lips so chapped I wanted to reach and peel off the dead skin.

Then she saw me. Her mouth grinned and she looked right at me, then turned her head to one side and peered up all sly and slantwise. Fluttered her lashes at me and it was godawful. I knew she wasn't crazy, but what the hell would anyone looking think? The nurse stopped combin and shook her head sayin tsk tsk tsk. She stood up with her bowl and knocked a signal on the door to be let out.

Once we were alone, Clarice sat on her bed, sorta slumped up against the wall. "Okay, Mardou," she says—that was her nickname for me way before I used it to write <u>My Blues Ain't Like Yours</u>. It's a combination of my name and the French word for sweet.

My conclusion is that besides hearing and seeing me, which no one on the fence's other side should be able to, nothing is all that wrong with my sister's mind. We talked a good long while, and except for a couple little lapses of memory—like she can't recall anything happened Friday—she functions perfectly.

And she desperately wants out. She even tried to grab my hand as I left, though I told her I'd be back soon. Didn't work; she couldn't touch me in the least. I oughta been worried it would, though, seeing as she saw right where I was. But I have my theory. I think it's cause I wasn't wearing that pendant from Leo, which I took off when he made me so mad at lunch.

What had happened Friday? Something so bad she blocked it out?

I climbed back this side of the fence once I got clear of the hospital. On the beach, actually, which was kinda risky without any cover. If anyone was watching I must have seemed to magically appear out of nowhere. But I had a longing to be near the water, and I looked around careful first.

Now I'm at home and wondering how to pull off a rescue mission if I'm gonna need to. When Leo gave me that special cross was the only time I brought someone with me outside. Pretty sure that's what made the difference. So the question will be, can I bring Clarice along if I can stand to wear it?

October 9 1963   Lunch with Marian. I took her to the Pen & Pencil in the Village for steak. At her insistence we rode the subway, which saved maybe ten minutes.

And ten dollars, sure, but what do I care about money anymore?

Marian seemed all moody on the train, then wouldn't tell me what was wrong till we had sat and ordered. She's fired. Boss caught her workin on her dyke magazine on company equipment and the company's dime, gave her till the end of the day to clear out her desk. If it was me, I'd have been a lot less worried about ending lunch on time. Well, I went with her after paying our bill and helped her pack her things, which may be the only reason they even let her back in. They know Julian's people. We took Marian's box—she had a cactus, a couple figurines, framed photos of the family and Daddy, and an empty scotch bottle to tote—to the flat she shares with her latest girlfriend, and I went on to Mama's.

It was not a good day for her, either. There's always the "Arthuritis," which is variable. And also sometimes she can't see too well. That did not stop her stubbornly going to the bathroom by herself, and since I ain't always there anyway, I let her. But while I was leaving a present in an envelope on the windowsill by her bed where she couldn't miss it, I saw another letter about Clarice. It was on top of a pile of papers stacked on a corner of the plant shelf Mama uses for a nightstand. I don't like to sneak, but this was Clarice.

Very official stationery with the South Beach address and phone number and everything on it, and saying how they had started the course of ECT early. That day. Friday. The day missing from her memory. I have been researching this topic, reading a book Dr. Dee loaned me. ECT stands for Electro-Convulsive Therapy. Electroshock. It is not always that great for the patient.

I heard Mama come thumping down the hall and put what I was reading back where I found it. I don't know whether I fooled her.

October 10 1963   Okay, maybe Leo is worth something. He will still travel the country back and forth at the drop of a baseball cap. He asked what he could do to get in bed with me again, and I said go to San Francisco where he last wrote from and find Rafael. Expecting him to refuse. And he hung his head down like a boxer, stuffed his hands in his jacket pockets, shuffled his feet around on the carpet in the hallway outside our apartment and said yes.

Will I keep my promise? We'll see when he gets back. He is leaving Friday with Roy. They're still friends, and they had been talkin for months about doin this anyway. Like the old days, but they'll drive instead of thumb rides this time.

So he says.

I gave him the name and number of Mr. Smallwood at Open Books and suggested the idea of doing a reading there. By his face, he hated it. But I think to make it with me again he would. Could be he goes. Tomorrow.

Tomorrow is also the day Julian comes home.

And tomorrow is when my sister receives her second treatment. I'm going to try to visit. See can I stop it somehow.

October 11 1963   No. No. That is <u>not</u> how they oughta be acting toward her. Nobody in the world is <u>that</u> crazy.

I went first thing in the morning, partly so I would be home when Julian came. He is still on the plane or probably landed and in customs by now, but nevermind because by the time I got to South Beach, it was already too late and they had sent her to I don't know what they call it and I don't care. Because it took till I left that woman's office to find out Clarice was not even in her room. And then she was.

Crying with snot running out of her nose—I mean, the orderly was wiping it off and blowing it, but was that just because of me being there? And her eyes blank and lids

He's here. Safe at home. We went out to The Palm— it was too early for supper but he was hungry and we held hands under the table covered in a checkered cloth. I couldn't eat and I had to say why.

First, I went into the trouble with Clarice. I felt all right asking him for her to stay with us when she got out. I could tell he didn't think it would be any time soon, but that's cool.

Next, I confessed Leo had called me and come around and I took him to lunch. Julian woulda found out anyway. Doorman woulda said, or somebody else. Besides, they used to be friends, too, and I actually met my husband through that same crowd. He knows how Leo never gave up even after we got married.

It was actually harder to talk about Rafael than Leo. By this time the waiter had taken away our plates and brought us ice cream for dessert—fancy vanilla with swirls of chocolate sauce and cherries and candied nuts on top. This I ate. Everything had come off swimmingly so far, but I wasn't sure if I was pushing my luck. I have never felt for any other man the way I will always feel for my angel Rafael.

So I tried to act like I was only tying up loose ends. Was that a lie?

Even feeling like I know I will forever, would I leave my husband for a man I haven't seen in eight years? Julian took my spoon away and pretended to steal my food, sayin I should have eaten it up faster.

Yes, his hair is yellow and his eyes are blue, but not the same blue as Rafael's, that blue so deep and so high I could start by falling into them and end up flying. And comfortable as Julian's arms felt when he hugged me and held me and pulled me down into our bed, and steady and calming as I find Julian's sleeping breaths, I had to get up and write in here how much I miss my angel.

October 12 1963   Columbus Day. There was a big parade. Julian is not Italian and me neither, but because of how it looks we had to go. Daddy's people didn't invite any of these white folks over here to this country, and Mama's people didn't ask them to bring any of her kin along to do their dirty work. I guess some good has come of it all, though. I mean I'm alive.

◻

October 13 1963   Riding back from church today with Mama I asked her outright would she release Clarice to my care. Instead of just hinting. "You don't want that, chile," she said. "What you need is to have yourself a baby. Even a mix one." I pointed out that was exactly what she'd done.

Mama smiled and patted my hand. Called me Little Tramp the way she used to call all us girls and reminded me Daddy wasn't white.

"Julian is Jewish," I told her, and she acted confused.

"That ain't white?"

According to Adam, who has the same background— and he's also not religious—it sorta is, sorta isn't. I preferred to talk about that idea than fend off demands for me to get pregnant. Got us to her door without arguing. I wasn't gonna come up but she insisted. Said she had something to show me.

It was a letter from South Beach. They were asking Mama's consent to give Clarice a lobotomy. To cut out a piece of her brain. And Mama was seriously considering it.

So then we fought. I get that she is remembering Daddy and how he never really recovered. But I think I convinced her to at least wait and put off any decision till another doctor could give his opinion. Which of course I expect to ask Dr. Dee this Wednesday, and his answer will be no.

October 14 1963   It's a sin, but I hate her. Hate hate hate her. Mama has sent Marian to jail.

Mama says it's Marian's fault since Marian was the one who committed the crime of distributing what they determined was lewd materials, but they would never have caught her. They would never have figured it out on their own. Like who was gonna guess "Maida Leaford" on the masthead meant Marian Todd? Who would have believed some colored woman calling herself after a character in Robin Hood?

But Mama remembered it from a game Marian used to play. When the preacher's wife came visiting and talking all scandalized about findin this copy of The Ladder in an apartment they rent out, Mama had to even the old-lady-gossip score with her and told her Marian's secret name for herself. Then acted surprised when the wife told the preacher and the preacher told the cops.

Julian has gone down to the station to throw Marian's bail and bring her here, since she and her girlfriend are kicked out of where they were living.

He's back. Alone. Says Marian and Loreena are moving into the Barbizon Plaza to be with "their community." Which apparently now includes whites if they're queers, too. Julian paid the first week's rent on top of Marian's bail, and he'll probably spring for a lawyer as well if she goes to trial.

He says I'm worth it. I say I know I am.

October 15 1963   Phone rang at four a.m. Julian answered it and handed it to me because it was Leo, who else? Long distance, from Chicago. I listened to him ramble on drunk for two whole minutes before I could squeeze a word in. All he wanted to talk about was could I wire him some cash to St. Louis so he and Roy could spend the night in a motel there and have dinner with some of Old Carmody's family the next day. Why were they doin that? He didn't get around to sayin, and I was too busy tryin to tell him my own troubles to ask.

Finally gave in. "HOW MUCH?" I practically shouted, and that caught his attention.

"Two hummer." He couldn't even pronounce it straight. Two hundred dollars.

Julian had been watching me, and when I repeated the figure and looked a question at him, he closed his eyes but also nodded. He held out his hand, and I passed him the receiver back. He had a pad and pencil, and he wrote down the necessary details, nodding and saying yeah till he hung up. So generous. It's a lie Jews are stingy.

Marian's new place is small but nice. Just one bed and a sofa anyone they need to stay over can sleep on. Offices a couple floors down for a bunch of different clubs for different types of whatever, including the Mattachine Society, which has been putting out The Ladder. Very handy. Plan is to keep publishing more issues despite the obscenity charges.

Apparently, the hotel's managers don't care who their tenants go with, long as their money's good and they pay it in advance. While I was stopping by this pair of obvious queens came in—barely knocked. I don't wanna be like Mama, so I smiled and was gracious and took three of the tickets to their theatrical performance they were handing out. Said they were inviting "the whole gang—everybody up and down the hall." My sister has wound up right where she needs to be.

October 16 1963   As I hoped, Dr. Dee opposes giving Clarice a lobotomy. He wrote Mama a long letter explaining why. Took a big part of my session. I don't care. I'm bringing it over to her now. Easier than trying to bust my sister free with magic I don't completely understand.

October 17 1963   I have to write it. Because it's true. Mama's dead. She died yesterday. Mama's dead.

Mama's dead. I am in her empty apartment now. I went with her to Sydenham's emergency department in the ambulance. She opened her eyes while I was looking but with that breathing mask on she couldn't talk, but she tried.

By the time we got there, her eyes were shut again, and they had to start her heart by shocking it. Like she let them do Clarice. Then they took her away to operate they said, but in my opinion she was dead already. Breathing but dead. Mind gone.

They never brought her back.

Somebody musta called Julian because next thing I knew he had me in a cab headed home. My face tucked into his soft wool shoulder, I was heaving big sighs and shuddering, crying without tears. Upstairs he fixed me a drink I didn't ask for and held it steady to my mouth. That did me some good. I managed to pull myself together and figure out what next.

Marian hadn't put in a telephone in her new place yet, so I called the bulldyke paper's office and told them fetch her to speak with me. She took it calmly. I shouldn't have been surprised. She and Mama hadn't been close in a long time.

By that point it was late, like 10 p.m. This neighborhood is highly questionable so we agreed to meet here now, today. I drank some more, smoked some tea I had left over from years ago. Probably got a whole hour's sleep.

I have an emergency appointment with Dr. Dee tomorrow.

A few pages back I wrote how I am in Mama's empty apartment. But it is actually crammed full: shelves and boxes and chests of drawers spilling over with old magazines and newspapers and photographs. Dried flowers, souvenirs from her wedding. Clothes she didn't even fit in anymore. My old diaries I thought I lost. Junk like greasy old potholders, things I didn't realize she'd kept like that card Esther and I made her for Mother's Day—found that in one of her worn-out purses stuck behind her bed's headboard. About a dozen of them there—I was lying under her sheets and blankets when I spotted them and pulled out the first one I touched.

Money in there, too. I can't just throw everything away. I can't stand to look at it all either, though. I have started and stopped five times since I got here.

Key in the door.

October 18 1963   Marian is taking care of sorting through Mama's stuff since it doesn't bother her the way it does me. Doesn't make her want to ask questions Mama can't answer anymore.

Dreamed last night the way I did before I learned from Dr. Dee how to work my visions. Just wild. Darkness was swirlin me around, grabbin me, tossin me in through a hospital window and out through the door to our apartment building, swanning me over the pool of the fountain in Washington Square, layin me gentle on the grass by the gate to Paradise Alley. And constant behind the scenes I do believe I heard Mama's voice whispering my name, soft as forgiveness.

131

Wish it could be real.

"Define real," says Dr. Dee. Have to admire how he makes me think so differently about things. Per him per the New Bedford Rose, dreams are a kind of reality we don't completely understand. We have to assume they are made up outta our own thoughts, our actions, and be serious about observing them. Skip right to the Third Petal. Sounds like Leo's new <u>Book of Dreams</u> is appearin exactly when it ought to. He doesn't know how correct he can be sometimes.

As for me, I took heart in Dee's advice. Keep movin. Keep dreamin. Keep learnin the petals as they forever unfurl. Mama loved me. She always only wanted what was best for me and for all her girls. She was wrong about Clarice, but she died before that could come back to hurt her. And now I'm my sister's nearest kin I can fix things for good.

He called late again, but not ridiculously late this time. Only about midnight, and Julian and I were still up. Well, we were in bed but not asleep. Givin each other back rubs the way we do. The phone was on the nightstand by my side, so it was me answering it.

"Mardou?" Leo sounded younger somehow. Like a kid.

"Yeah?"

"Me and Roy just wanted to thank you for the money." I told him he was welcome and really he ought to be thanking my husband, not me.

"Screw that." He giggled when he said it, though, so I didn't think I had made him that mad. "Listen, next time can you send it—"

I sat up. "'<u>Next</u> time'? Ain't gonna <u>be</u> no next time!" I felt Julian's broad palms on my back, his long fingers soothing down my scrunched-up shoulders. Whispering shhh, shhh, shhh to cool my temper.

That was no good because of what Mr. Leo-Bestseller-Percepied said next: "Two hundred was enough to get us to New Orleans, but now we need to pay a deposit on the house we're renting."

I dropped my jaw and let loose of the receiver. Heard it hit the carpet like it was far away as Leo. No, farther. Far away as Rafael.

Squawking noises told me he was still talking. Saying what? That he had flat lied to me? That he had taken my money—my husband's money—to do what he damn well pleased when he surely had abundant resources of his own?

I flopped back down on the bed, pulled up the covers, and shut my eyes. As if I was going to be able to get back to sleep. The yammering on the phone stopped and a buzzing tone started in its place, and Julian left the bed and went around to hang the receiver in its cradle. Then he went outta the room. I lay there in the dark a while till I smelled coffee curling along the corridor and followed him into our kitchen. He had a pan of milk warming up on the gas, ready to pour in my cup. Another way Julian resembles my angel is how considerate and kind he can be.

We sat down together at the kitchen's little green-painted table and drank and talked. I told him what Leo had said and why it pissed me off. All he did was nod, and that made me pissed with him, too. Leo had stolen from us, but Julian wasn't gonna fly down there and knock him out? I mean there's gentle and there's firm, and why can't he be both?

October 19 1963   Mostly layin around today. Leo called again about four in the afternoon. Soon as I figured out it was him I hung up. Didn't answer the next two times the phone rang. Finally, there was a knock on the door: Western Union, with a telegram from my agent saying phone him at his office.

On a Saturday? Had to be important. So I dialed him up and it certainly was: Open Books had sent us an offer for publishing my poetry. Contingent on me movin out there while we work on it.

That's going to take some thinking. Talking and thinking.

◻

October 20 1963   I'm not surprised Julian supports the idea. He is always urging me on to be more independent of him, the way I was when we met. And I know I should be, and I'm getting to where mostly I am.

He could come see me in California if things took more than a month. How bad can it be? How long can it last?

Missing Mama something awful today. I would always see her Sundays to take her to church. When I first got up I was looking in my closet for what I would wear to services without even realizing it. Maybe if I accept Mr. Smallwood's offer, I'll get a chance to get over her. By being in some other city, I'll stop expecting to see her. I'll stop expecting she is only a cab ride away.

And my secret hope of finding Rafael could be realized if I go.

Could he somehow be behind this?

I have to decide soon. My agent says the plane ticket is for five days from now.

◻

October 21 1963   Funeral today. At that white church. Mama's body looked normal, which I guess indicates the funeral home Julian picked did a good job. He handled most of the details after I told him the main things I remember she wanted: for the service to be celebrated the same place where Daddy's was, play organ music, to be cremated, scatter her ashes off Staten Island.

I cried but I didn't collapse. Marian neither. Esther, who had got the day off from teaching and driven in from Wilmington, looked angrier than she did sad, which makes sense, seeing as she blamed me for coming between them.

Nothing from Wanda. No sign of her. Last anybody heard from her was years ago. Daddy's funeral.

After the service Julian invited everyone to our place for sandwiches he had ordered. I was tired so I went to bed soon as Marian and Esther left. Said they were going to Mama's to clean it up and sort things out.

How could my sisters be so <u>stupid</u>? How could they do something so wrong? How am I going to fix <u>this</u>?

Mailing a letter takes a couple of days. One day at least. Esther stamped the envelope and had Marian drop it in the box yesterday, but the mailman couldn't have picked it up till today. And with Mama dead nearly a week prior to the postmark, Clarice's lobotomy order has to be null and void.

Has to be. But do I trust them doctors and secretaries to pay proper attention to the details of some colored girl's treatment? I do not.

I'm going to have to revive my idea of breaking her out. Vague as it was. Is.

Under the circumstances I anticipate coming from that, it probably makes sense for me to leave town. So yes, I will be accepting the Open Door's offer and taking advantage of their airplane ticket.

Now to set up my sister's escape.

October 22 1963   I need to get a better handle on what I'm doin. That's got to help me get my sister free.

Dr. Dee has taught me so much, but even he admits this kind of working is tricky. I talked with him about it one whole session, complained how things changed, constantly, how I went outside from the stage that time at the Cedar without meaning to, how at Adam's there were these little doors or windows in the magic's mist, how once in a while I could go through walls but floors held me up, and did any of that make sense? How can I learn the rules if they keep changing?

According to him, we make up our own rules our own selves. If that's true, how come I don't know them by heart before they happen?

All right. Applying the Rose. My Thought is that if I write my rules out they will stabilize for me. So.

> 1. I go outside when I want to, but also when I need to get away from anything awful, and also when I need to find something that that's the only way it can be found.
>
> 2. Just certain special people can do it. Partly because this is a genetic ability, one possessed by me and Clarice, for example. Probably by Daddy,

139

too? But there have to be a few other strains as well, because Dr. Dee is not related. Not closely, anyway.

3. I can take people with me, but only if I am wearing that Cross of Lorraine Leo gave me. I hate this one, but I think it's right. My feeling of recognition for it sparked my curiosity, and I did some research. Like he was saying, those French resistance fighters used it for their symbol, but there are also a few older associations. One I keyed in on was the image of a horse carrying two knights—which you can see in it when you turn it sideways and squint. So I will wear it again this time.

It worked! Too tired for any more.

October 23 1963   About yesterday. First time I have ever deliberately moved somebody else over the fence! I went outside like before, by the intersection of Seaview and

Magnolia, soon as Julian had left for his office. In the hospital, I followed the Thought of her again and found my sister lying on an uncomfortable-looking table with wheels. Seemed to be some sort of hallway.

Clarice's head was bald, her gorgeous hair shaved off completely, which I took to be a very bad sign as well as ugly. They were goin ahead with the procedure, and I was in the nick of time. Preparations had already begun. Not sedated yet, though—her eyes were open, and when I went up and hung over her face, I could tell she saw me. So I started talking, betting she could hear me, too, like last time. I warned her not to say anything back, but she just laughed and said by now they were sure she was crazy.

Next part of my plan is why I was wearing the pendant and why I pulled it out of my sweater on its chain and put it in my sister's hand. Why she could grab hold of me. The Cross was our horse. We were the knights.

We rode on out of there like Lee Morgan playing "Tom Cat": sassy. Saucy. So bad, so sure, so free. Mists parted, walls vanished, streets led us to the sand, to the

141

sea. To the breakers with their white manes tossin as they galloped up to greet us. As they swirled around our feet, as I kissed my sister hello and goodbye. As they carried her off to a window opening just then on another land, another sky. Where she wanted to be. Her new home.

That wasn't the outcome I had intended, but Clarice has her own mind. She squeezed my hand and said she'd see me soon and left me behind on the beach.

Or anyway, that's the story I'm writing in here. Can't nobody tell me it would hold up in a court of law, neither. Cops ever look at this book they will only see practice pieces for my fairy tales. Cause that's all they <u>can</u> be. Officially.

Officially, I got the phone call today that Clarice had wound up missing. Checking with me to see had she shown up here before they reported it to the police.

Like the police will care.

October 24 1963   Flying out tomorrow. I had asked Julian to reserve a seat next to mine on the airplane for Clarice to sit in, but it turns out that's not necessary.

Apparently, some policeman or another <u>does</u> care about what happened to my sister because two detectives came by to talk to me. I made em wait down in the lobby while I put on my best, most bridge club-looking dress and hat and jacket. Answered their "routine" inquiries as if I had not a care in the world—till the one, the older one with the mustache, mentioned Marian.

"Why yes, that's our sister, too." I acted surprised he knew her name. "Well, really Clarice is my and Marian's half-sister by the same father." Then I spent a good while explaining more than they wanted to hear about Mama and Daddy and the ins and outs of their marriage. Couldn't stop me till I glanced at my wristwatch and uttered my most ladylike non-swear words: "My gracious heavens! I'll be late!"

I got nearly to the door, but the younger one ran and stepped in my way. Asked me if I had any idea where he could reach Marian. I told him the hotel name but made

143

like I had forgot which room number. Let them waste their time and energy talkin to the Mattachines and so forth. That'll give Marian some kind of warning they're on her trail.

October 25 1963   I love flying on an airplane! My first time on my own, and while they may have treated me better when I went with Julian, today I had the window <u>and</u> the aisle seats to myself! Food wasn't so great: cold rolls and hard butter? And the chicken was on the dry side. But the wine was fine. Good thing we got in only four hours after takeoff or I would be sloshed.

It is strangely light here. Time difference, I guess: should be 9 but California clocks say it's only 6. Day for night.

October 26 1963   Not even a hotel, but this Villa Rosa Motel is supposed to be the most elegant of its variety ever. I knew better than to try the Palace or one of them grand downtown places, and when I realized Villa Rosa is walking distance—less than a mile—from Open Books, I had Julian book me in here. I could tell they were a little surprised Mrs. Starr was a Negro, but this being North Beach they mostly managed to cover that up. Mostly.

Store opened at 11. I went in with the first customers: a few seedy-looking old ladies buyin newspapers in French, Polish, and Russian; couple of blear-eyed, bearded boys smellin like fish and fresh bread; a Chinese woman who zipped down the stairs ahead of me as if I was out to steal a jump on whatever books of wisdom she was zeroed in on. Mr. Smallwood's office was in the store's basement, but the door painted to say "I Am That I Am" was shut and the handle in it didn't even turn. Locked.

So I waited and browsed around. Signs marked off sections with names like "Muckraking" and "Evidence." The suspicious Chinese woman was in "Stolen Continents," building a short stack of books on the linoleum.

When I finally heard his office door open, I gave the man a minute to settle himself in, then went over and knocked on it—even though it wasn't quite shut. He knew who I was right away. Wanted me to do a reading soon as he could get me in the papers. I agreed so he would stop talking about it and brought us around to our ostensible main topic: publishing my collection. I had a briefcase full of typed poems—copies, because why would I risk carrying around the only ones existed?

He fought me a little on using a pseudonym. My agent is firm on the point, though, and Dr. Dee supports his insistence. Lucius gave in. We're going with the same author name as <u>My Blues Ain't Like Yours</u>, despite the fact that Leo has basically igged it so far and sales are going nowhere. "Marlene Todd's" kids' books are doing way better, but that's no reason to confuse folks about what they're in for when they buy this.

We set an appointment for Tuesday so he has time to read what I've written. He asked me what I think the title should be, and I had his answer immediately: <u>Nightdreamer.</u>

At last we were done with business. I pretended to be casual about it and found out my angel's address. A

P.O. Box, like Lucius had said on the telephone, but I managed to learn which station.

October 27 1963   I went despite the fact that it's Sunday. Yes, it's closed, but it's so nearby. I like the little park this post office fronts on. Plenty of shrubbery it will be easy for me to duck behind when I go outside and come back. No one's gonna see me vanish and reappear.

A short walk and I returned to my room, glad to get in from the wind. This motel is supposed to have a sauna, which will be nice and warm. Villa Rosa is so modern. Big windows, tub, and a phone in every room. Before I hit the sauna I'll call Julian again. It's five o'clock in NYC. He should be back from wherever he went by now.

They wanted to arrest Marian. Again. Again! For murder!

I am completely calm and collected. Everything is under control, and Julian got her released from the interrogation room because she was smart enough to call him. Or maybe she thought she was calling me. Doesn't matter. She's back at the Barbizon, he says, upset, understandably, that they thought she was capable of killing Clarice, but otherwise she's fine.

I don't need to go home. Man, I would, but Julian absolutely insists it's not necessary. I believe him, especially since he promised me Marian said so, too, and he gave me her number. Going to call now.

See this is the kind of trick police like to pull. They did not even dare to charge Marian with a crime, just asked her all these questions about the way she drove Clarice crazy trying to convert her to "tribadism." Claimed they had some—nonexistent—letters for proof, but for proof of what? No body, so no murder has taken place. Think because we're spades we're stupid.

◻

October 28 1963   Today I braved the beach. Sun was shining till I crossed Hyde Street, and like that the clouds rolled in. They call it fog around here, but if this was fog, it was high enough that I could see blocks ahead and either side. Beach was to my right. So I turned off onto the grass and then the sand, where the fog was hanging low, like I'm used to. And there she was. Standin ankle-deep in the water and wearin nothin but a smile. Her hair had grown long again like it was spozed to be. In only six days, somehow. She beckoned me to her. I stepped forward and outside.

"Hey, Sis." She said it like it was normal for her to be here on the other end of the country from where I left her. And naked. I guess no one else could see her, though. If we were followin my rules.

I said hey back. She reached for my hand and took hold of it—I was wearing Leo's Cross like I do every day now, hoping to be beside her again. Still, I know I looked confused as I felt to find her <u>here</u>. And worried, maybe? There weren't a lot of people around because, I mean, it was a weekday in October, but there were a few. Walking

149

dogs or trudging along like that was their job. What if she climbed back by mistake to the side of the fence where anyone could see her? Without no clothes on?

My sister asked me what was wrong, and I glossed over all that quick as I could for the main questions: Where had she been? What kind of place was it? Did she like it? Was she going to ever want to climb back over?

Sounded as if where she had traveled to, her mama was a movie queen. And they lived in a mansion on a tropical island. For her, this had been seven months, not just seven days, but she was not even a little homesick. In raptures about fresh ripe fruit and juicy fish and beautiful flowers spreading perfume everywhere and talking with parrot-colored bears. ... I believed her, but that didn't keep me from wishing she'd go back with me now instead of seeming further and further away with every description.

Sun came out. Didn't help me see her any better. In fact it made things worse—the light washed Clarice thin like she was painted with leftover paints. "You really here?" I asked her.

She laughed. "Really where? I can meet you any place land meets sea."

"I mean, is this really you? Your body?"

"Yeah, it's mine!" But soon as she said that, she faded away more. "And I am ready to get my body back to what I was doin before. Goodbye!"

What had she been doing that was so important? "Wait!" I yelled. I was yelling at the empty air. Clarice was gone. No window even. Guess she was inventing new rules.

I climbed back over the fence alone.

Golden sparkles on the water told me time had been passing faster than I felt since I went outside. While the sun was still bright, it had sunk a lot lower. I turned and waded to shore, found my socks and shoes under the newspaper by the trash barrel where I had stashed them, put them on. Then I left before it got actually late.

I bought a sandwich from a gas station and went and sat and ate it in the park facing the post office. My angel

151

never came. Just some bossy squirrel who wanted my crusts.

When I got back to my room and called Julian he didn't answer. But it was only 9 at night there. Or 10. I could try again in a little while. Then the phone rang and I was sure it must be him.

No, it was not. Goddam Leo.

Leo had a favor to ask me. The goddam nerve. Would I endorse his movie. In exchange, he said he was willing to finally promote my book. Not <u>Nightdreamer</u>—he doesn't even know I'm doing that one. He meant <u>My Blues</u>.

"What movie?" I asked him. Only thing I had heard about was this sorta goofy half-lies production some student had scammed him and Adam and Roy into making. They called it "Pull My Daisy," and you know what they meant by that. This one was new, Hollywood, based on a stupid story he wrote about him and me. I hate that book. I'm betting I'll hate the movie more.

Partly to get rid of Leo and free up the phone line, partly because I knew my agent would scold me if I didn't, I agreed. As I hung up I heard him thanking me and jabbering something about some (white) French actress playing the lead. Playing me.

So be it.

October 29 1963   Today was my meeting with Mr. Lucius Smallwood. You would think by now this publishing stuff would be easy for me. There's always something new, though. Always.

Like this time it was about "formatting." Poems that didn't fit all on the same page we had to decide where they "broke," where they ought to leave off and start up again. We also had to pick their order. The order I had put them in wasn't always the best for the book's "flow," meaning arranging it so when the breaks happened the poem's two parts appeared on facing pages. I learned so much.

Open Books uses the same cover design for everything. We didn't have that to argue over.

He thought I should ask Adam to help me out. Talk about the book to his friends, teachers studying him, newspapers and magazines writing articles on his work. I said I'd give it a shot.

Went by the park when we were finished. Still no sign of my angel coming to pick up his mail.

Checked at the motel's office on my way in. Still no word from Julian. I'm starting to worry.

October 30 1963   I saw him. My angel. We talked. Today.

I went in the morning. That was the key. He was waiting on the bottom one of the building's three short steps before the doors unlocked. I climbed the fence and went up next to him, where he would have seen me if I hadn't been outside. He seemed to sense something anyway, turning his longlashed eyes to where I moved.

The doors opened and he went in the lobby to his box where my letter was waiting for him. I know exactly what he read. I had kept a copy and packed it and brought it with me.

He liked what I'd written, I could tell. Didn't smile, but the little wrinkles above his eyebrows relaxed, like I remember them doing when I would lie there stroking his forehead, hungry for his sweetness. He crumpled up the paper like he was gonna throw it away. Instead, he held it to his nose and breathed in deep. Trying to catch a whiff of my scent!

I groaned. I couldn't stand it. My angel.

I followed him out the front. Through the park and a little ways down Powell Street. In a low door, up a flight of high stairs to what I recognized must be his apartment. Looked like it should be his: hardly any furniture except this short-legged Japanese table with cushions around it on the floor. Sleek grey cat stalked in from the other room and saw me and sat down to stare.

Yeah, I was busted. Rafael directed his gaze to the same spot the cat was looking and called my name: "Mardou?" My sisters' nickname for me Leo stole. My pen name. I wasn't going to say anything. Got up to leave, to spend a day thinking. Draw a new Rose.

But then he put out his hand, and it was shaking. Said my name again soft. I had to stay.

He kept gazing my direction while he dug out a candle, matches, and a joint from a cookie tin. While he lit them. While he took a drag off the joint and blew it out. While he spoke.

"I know you're here, Mardou; I feel you. Come to track me down? Don't worry. I'm not gonna say anything. Julian's safe."

Which was strange—of course my husband was safe. Why shouldn't he be? Curiosity pulled at me to climb back over to Rafael's side of the fence and find out. But before I could do that he was outside, too. With me.

Dee is right. We make our own rules, because, now my angel had put hisself out there next to me, the rules were changing to reflect some part of him: the normal mists began to shimmer, like pearls in sunlight, and we were floating above the floor, not standing on it. That felt weird but also as if I had done it before.

Rafael said my name again, this time firmly, like a prayer he already knew was answered. Held out his hand again, steady this time, and I held out mine. We touched, and I felt <u>something</u>. Not the warm, rough skin I remember from before; not the old callouses and new scars I saw by the pearly mist. No. It wasn't the same as with Clarice.

What I felt was so light. A touch a little like feathers. Just enough to tell me he was there.

That wasn't all he told me.

Long story short, he had gone over the fence—or rather done his version of that, what he calls "walking between"—when he disappeared eight years ago. And he disappeared because he was being framed for killing somebody. And that framing was done by Leo and Carmody and Roy. And the real killer was my husband. Julian.

October 31 1963   Hallowe'en. I remember us girls would dress up like scarecrows and hoboes and whatever characters we could put together from stealing clothes outta Mama's sewing work. Wonder if

I want to, but I'm not ready to completely believe what Rafael said yesterday. Surely, he made a mistake about my husband killing some poor man, even if it was accidentally. And I bet my angel got blamed mainly because cops are so stupid. Though I also bet Leo really did have something to do with misleading them. ... But then what does it mean that my husband proposed to me hardly two weeks after this supposedly went on?

I know why I accepted Julian's proposal: because my angel up and vanished. I was thinking Julian was as close to him as I would ever get—though I didn't feel proud about thinking that. But now I'm worried I know the reason why he wanted me as his wife. It was not for love. It was in case that death was ever brought to trial. I would not be able to testify against Julian if I we were married. I would not be able to poke a hole in his fake alibi.

An O.D. That's an accident, right? No matter who provided the dope? No matter what condition the body is in when it's found?

Okay. So here's what I'm gonna ask when I finally have Mr. Julian Starr on the telephone: Did you do it? Did you mean to? And did you fix things so someone else took the fall for you or was that Leo's fault? Any regrets afterwards?

I dialed five times. No one answered. At last I phoned up Marian and got her to go over there and call me with what she found out. Waiting.

He's gone. There was a note. Short and sorry.

Julian had found Rafael's book Dr. Dee gave me and figured his time was running out before he would be exposed. So he has split somewhere they can't bring him back.

He left plenty money in our checking account, he said.

I guess I know now who was telling how much of the truth.

November 2 1963   All Souls Day. Mama became more interested in this as a holiday once she joined a church named for it. According to Dr. Dee, we're at one of the times of year it's the easiest to slip outside and come back in again. Curtains dividing it from the world are extra thin right now. Fence is low to climb.

I talked to Marian a little more last night. She knew the name of the man who Julian had killed: Thaddeus Cameron. Papers wrote it up as random violence. Translation: they didn't know who killed him and they didn't care. Just another beat-to-death queer who most likely got what he deserved for makin indecent advances. Or whichever people believed it was Rafael to blame cared even less. Let the homos get rid of one another without causin the slightest amount of inconvenience to anyone else.

Naturally, Marian's friends thought differently.

There's some pent up disgust about it that is going to drive them into action fairly soon.

I don't wanna dwell on how the man got marked up like they found him. Whose idea that musta been. Who did it.

This morning I walked from Villa Rosa to my angel's apartment, loving every light pole and telegraph line on my way. To think of him being so close! I brought us cinnamon rolls from the grocery market, and he brewed us more of his special tea I remember from Paradise Alley with all its right ingredients. We took our cups and rolls to the playground across the street, like a picnic.

Sun was shining so bright it might as well be spring. Stiff breeze cut through the illusion, though. We huddled into each other grinning, gulped up the tea before it cooled too far down. I'm not shy. I wrapped my arms around his shoulders. "Ready to go?" I asked.

He was shocked. "Go outside? Here? How?" Said we needed that candle he had lit yesterday. Said we had to be high. Said we had to concentrate, meditate, couldn't

161

just jump outside, climb the fence like I been doin year on year.

I showed him how wrong he was. Took him over with me, then told him, too; quoted Dr. Dee. My rules. Then we experimented with some of his. I learned a few new things.

For instance, a speedier way to travel. It's a fiercer version of how I found my sister in the mental hospital: putting yourself on the fastest route to someplace by focusing on the presence of someone who's there. Sort of like you're throwing yourself into this high, still wind— that's the best I can do to describe how it works.

But it does work. That's why I know Julian went to Venezuela. Me and Rafael did, too, and there he was, crossing the lobby of some swanky big city hotel. He appeared a bit tired but otherwise fine. A little sad. Did he miss me? I didn't climb over to his side to ask.

Managing the return trip had me stumped for a moment. With my angel beside me, who did I want to be with that badly who was still in San Francisco? But

Rafael knew what to do: he sent us in search of his cat, Sealy. We finished our excursion right inside Rafael's front door. We curled up together, warm on top of the covers.

November 3 1963   What am I going to do? It's seven in the morning. I should still be sleeping. Instead, I'm awake and writing. Not many more pages remain in this journal, though my heart is spilling over with feelings. They are simply not going to fit.

So just the facts. Julian has left me for good. Clearly. Not only did my angel and I spot him half a globe away. When I came back from Rafael's apartment there was a fat yellow envelope waiting for me at the motel's front desk. It was stuffed full of papers. I stayed up all night reading them and trying to understand what they were saying. At least twice I have given up. It's going to take a lawyer, and how will I find one in a strange city? On a Saturday?

■

I called Marian. Loreena answered, but then they both had ideas about who in SF could help. Marian reminded me to plot a Rose. I'll have to use the motel's stationery and stick it in here loose.

At least I will have plenty of money, a big allowance, I guess. Long as I don't tell anybody who really killed Thaddeus Cameron. That's the main sense I get outta all these documents.

Which leads to my dilemma. How else besides telling on Julian can I make it so my angel's free? He is renting his place with a fake name—criminals he knows from hustling in the neighborhood around the Black Hawk have hooked him up with the necessary I.D.

That would not have been cheap, and he's still scared to risk going anywhere he might be recognized, like the Village. Could I do better for him with my allowance? What's the best protection, money or the truth?

And what's my proof? Jabber by somebody a bestselling author calls a bum and a jailbird. Somebody accused of the same murder. Leo's fans are not going to want to believe he had anything to do with covering this up, either.

But is it right that the man who's responsible for Thaddeus Cameron's death gets off scot-free? But what good is justice? The man is dead and he's gonna stay dead.

These aren't facts. Let me stick to those.

Yesterday afternoon, while we were lying beside each other, I told Rafael about rescuing Clarice and seeing her Sunday at the beach and how for now she wanted to remain over the fence. He said he had spent some time outside himself, hiding, and got excited at the idea that my sister might know more about it, stuff he could learn from her. Despite that, it has only been a week-and-a-half since I broke her free of that mental hospital. Time is funny outside, which he, of course, knew and reminded me of.

The upshot is that when I go to see him again today we have plans to climb over and look for Clarice. She will guide us and help me and him decide what to do next, because she will be familiar with that space, that time, that dream. She'll show us everything we want to see and give us ideas: shut up about the murder? Or lie? Or swear the truth? Stay on this side of the fence and publish my book of poems? Or go? Or both?

One thing I'm sure of: Rafael and I are going to be rich, whichever way we work things. Because if no one knows that what you have exists, they can't steal it.